PRINCESS
AWAKENING

Princess Awakening

TOWER OF SAND

L.A. Soria

Protagonist Press

Published by
Protagonist Press
Bellingham, WA
www.Protagonist.press

First Printing—December 2020
23 22 21 20   4 3 2 1

Acknowledgments: This story first appeared in serialized chapters published by the author on Medium.com. Some of the Latin text is taken from the Latin Vulgate translation of the Bible, which is in the public domain. The Italian verse is from "Canticle of the Sun," which was written by Saint Francis of Assisi and is in the public domain. Though the faces and places of the story do correspond with historical research, they are entirely works of fiction.

Cover art by Courtney Clay
Cover design by Nathaniel Soria

Library of Congress Cataloging-in-Publication Data
  Soria, L.A.
   Princess Awakening: Tower of Sand—1st ed.
   1. Fiction—Fantasy 2. Fiction—Historical
  Library of Congress Control Number: 2020922650

ISBN 978-1-7361346-0-3
eBook ISBN 978-1-7361346-1-0

Contents

AD 1225

The Free Country, West Francia

1

Is the Devil a Woman?

Aurelie woke to the touch of a cold hand brushing across her face. The fingers fumbled, hesitating, as if the hand itself loathed the touch. Then soft flesh pressed down over her nose and mouth.

Aurelie repressed a scream.

She wanted to jerk away and beat back the limp, invasive thing, but she did not. She had recognized that touch, the hesitancy and the fragility of it. And she sensed the rank smell of stress and sweat under too many layers, too many oils. Her second impulse, the trained one, was to hold still and protect this unwanted visitor by doing nothing at all and receiving whatever came next—good or ill.

"Maman?" she whispered in the dark.

In answer, the fingers slid down across her lips once, then pulled away. Thin streams of moonlight bled through the stained-glass window, dimly lighting the pale blue dress of shimmering silk, the white wimple, the frozen silhouette of the queen. Behind her, the tower door gaped open.

Aurelie's breath caught in her throat.

"Get up, quietly," Queen Yolande said, her girlish whisper sounding like a hiss.

A cold draft from the open door blew across Aurelie's face, and she hesitated. She could hear the gentle snores of Sera, wrapped tightly in the yellow woolen blanket and sleeping, as always, with her frayed wimple still knotted around her face. Aurelie longed to roll into her old friend and stay huddled in the warmth, under the blanket. But everyone in the castle had a role to play, and it was Aurelie's duty to obey. She rose out of the low pallet that was her bed and stood, waiting for the queen to state her will.

"Go," Queen Yolande whispered, and she pointed to the blackness beyond the open door.

A tremor passed through Aurelie. She reached for her clothes, folded neatly on the floor, and she placed each garment on the bed, hoping the queen could not see the trembling of her brown hands in the darkness. The queen, her mother, lived by a code of rules. One was never to come fully inside the tower room. The other was never to let Aurelie out. So, in this moment, Aurelie guessed, the queen was breaking the rules for a very important reason. And that was probably to save Aurelie's life—or to end it.

Aurelie smoothed out the undershirt she already wore, a little too short for her tall frame, too tight across her curves, but still soft and familiar. White linen. Three hundred and thirty-six stitches. Aurelie had counted every one of them, though she had never seen a needle in her life, let alone touched one. She picked up her next layer, the embroidered chemise, also linen, cream colored. One thousand, two-hundred and twelve stitches. She eased the fitted garment over her head and straightened it over her hips. She would love to imagine that her mother was just taking her out of the tower for the first time ever on the judgment day of her legendary curse simply for the purpose of wishing Aurelie well and helping her to prepare for her introduction to the kingdom and the party ahead. In that imaginary scene, this mother would loop arms lovingly with that daughter and confide how she herself had once-upon-a-time come of age and fallen in love with King Hugh of the Free Country and how she had decided to leave the elegant courts of her home in Aquitaine to rule with him over the wild, free mountains and people of the Jura.

But that vision was of another mother.

Or another daughter.

Ones the Devil had not yet marked.

Aurelie reached for her overtunic, her favorite garment, a sleeveless, loose-fitted dress of beet-pink wool that belled gracefully from the waist. Seven-hundred and eighty-one stitches. Aurelie had a choice to make, and she knew that simple obedience was not her only option. It was her own life at stake, after all—her destiny. And she did not like the idea of playing the pawn in other people's games. As Sera would say, the chessboard nearly always held at least one more move. For one thing, Aurelie could feign a coughing fit right now and wake Sera. That way, at least, someone would bear witness to whatever was coming next—whatever that might be. But then the queen would be angry, and Sera would fret. Aurelie would probably leave alone with the queen anyway. And Sera would remain here awake, grieved and worried.

Aurelie pulled the dress over her head. In truth, part of her actually wanted to leave now with the queen. She had always longed to leave the tower. Of course, she had imagined going out safely after the curse had ended. But, no matter how many plans she made in her heart, as Bishop Aimery would say, "Voluntas autem Domini permanebit." What's more, even if Aurelie did find a way to stay in the tower, she wasn't guaranteed safety. Similarly, she could leave now and still live through the dangerous day ahead with all the use of her heart, mind and strength to defend herself. This was not going to be the last choice she would ever make.

The wind outside blew forcefully against the sandstone tower, and Aurelie imagined that she could feel the structure shaking under her feet. She glanced at her mother, still as a statue.

What would a princess do? Aurelie wondered. That was the real question. What choice must the future leader of the Free Country make? The thought warmed her, kindling the fire that always burned inside. She reached for her leather belt and strapped it around her hips. First, of course, a princess had to look good. Second, she had to uphold her family's honor. And third, she had to be ready to serve her people—even at the sacrifice of herself. Aurelie tried not to dwell on that last duty. Right now, she had a chance to seize her destiny early, to see what the real world looked like up close, to meet her kingdom and become known. So what if the path seemed dangerous and unexpected? If she had only one day left to live, she wanted to live it outside of the tower. Aurelie smiled to herself as she slid her leather shoes over her feet. Why not?

She took a step, then, on impulse, reached down for one more item—a book. Her hand steadied as it gripped the stiffened pages of bound leather. This could provide a kind of shield, she figured, in case she needed more than her heart and mind to defend herself. Then she moved to the open doorway, stopped before the dark threshold and looked back.

Each massive stone of that round, sandstone room had been cut and placed just for her, and she felt reluctant to leave it this way. The bed had given her rest. The fireplace had kept her warm. The books and chess set had grown her mind. And the stained-glass window had offered her beauty. Aurelie's eyes fell on Sera, curled up and snoring like the soft rumble of thunder in the hills, and Aurelie's heart ached, realizing this could be the last time she would ever look upon her friend and companion of so many years. But she also knew that Sera would be safer here without her. *Thank you for everything, ma bonne amie,* Aurelie said silently in her heart. Then she told herself to be brave and stepped across the threshold.

The air felt colder on the landing at the top of the spiraling staircase, and the way in front of Aurelie faded into a blackness she could not see beyond. A church bell clanged in the city, and she jumped, counting the tolling of the bell. Midnight. The beginning of the name day of her sixteenth year—the very last day of her cursed life. Aurelie felt a brush of cold metal against her hand, and time slowed, severing in thoughts and visions and bursts of light. Terror gripped her heart, and she jumped away and swiveled around, opening her mouth to scream, but she saw only her mother, squeezing in behind her on the landing. An impossibly disloyal and agonizing thought took hold of Aurelie's mind—that her mother, her own mother, held in her hand the instrument of her daughter's betrayal. Aurelie took a step back, almost falling down the stair.

The queen was swinging the tower door shut, raising her double-headed key to the lock, sliding it in and turning it.

Then Aurelie heard a familiar clink, and she recognized the sound. The cold metal she'd felt brush her hand was not a weapon but a key—one of the many keys that the queen always wore belted around her waist. Everything fit back into place, neatly explainable, non-threatening. Almost. Aurelie gulped, gasping in air, and the sound echoed in the closed space. She tried to believe there was a simple explanation to everything happening to her in this moment. There was no danger to fear. But complete blackness enclosed her, and she felt sick with dizziness. She wanted to grab hold of someone or something, but she dared not grab her own frail mother for fear that she would crush her or be crushed.

"Don't misstep," Queen Yolande whispered from behind. "The stairs are steep and narrow. If you trip, you could fall all the way down."

Aurelie flinched at the feel of the queen's breath on her face, the hissing whisper so close to her ear. Aurelie slid a foot forward till she felt the edge of the first step. Then she forced her foot to keep moving. The step down felt weird, bottomless, demanding too much trust. Her head reeled. Thirty-three steps—that was how many times she had to move her feet down to get out of here. She had listened to other feet walk these steps over and over across the years. She had dreamed of leaping or dancing down them one day. But now her stomach knotted, and her head spun. She closed her eyes and took another step down, reminding herself that she was a princess. She had to live beyond walking down a set of stairs in the dark.

At twenty-five steps, she saw a sliver of light leaking through a cracked door, and she finished the stairs in a rush and pushed through the door. Two guards waited in the corridor, one holding a torch, and Aurelie sidestepped, moving away from them. She scanned their faces, tired and blank, dutifully averted. She knew most people at the castle by stance and by gait—the things she could understand best from looking out of her high window. Up close, these men looked surprisingly pocked and whiskered and blotchy. The load of new details overwhelmed her. She could not place them or distinguish their characters from such a surplus of new information, and she looked away. Granite walls. Torchlight. Cobwebs. Dust. She glanced down at the book clutched in her hand: *Mundus iste totus quoddam scaccarium est*, the title read—*The World is a Kind of Game of Chess*. Aurelie grimaced.

"Bonsoir messieurs," she whispered, and to her own ears, her voice sounded too soft, too gentle.

The men startled and glanced up, then quickly looked away again. "Bonsoir your highness," they answered. One covered his eyes.

Aurelie wondered if they, too, were surprised or disappointed by the person they saw in front of them. Her father had always called her remarkable. "Skin like the golden-brown color of the finest myrrh of Sheba," he would say. "Hair as lush as the dark woods of the Jura itself. Mind as sharp as the sages of Zagwe." But King Hugh was a doting father. Maybe these guards saw only a cowering woman, too sheltered and too scared to be the future leader of their country. Aurelie lifted her chin, trying to rise above her nervous thoughts. "Thank you for coming here to protect me," she said, speaking with a little more strength and volume.

The guards looked at each other and did not answer.

Queen Yolande stepped out of the tower, and they straightened, their eyes avoiding her face, too. Torchlight hit her fair, scallop-shell colored skin with harsh lines of light and shadow. A long, bone hairpin jutted sharply across the side of her head, binding her wimple over her chin and forehead. Not a single strand of hair was visible besides her thin red eyebrows. She looked small and fragile in this dark corridor next to these armed men. And she also looked dangerous.

A yearning stirred in Aurelie's heart, a desire for connection, for repair. "Maman," she whispered, "is everything all right? What are we doing here?"

Queen Yolande flinched and opened her mouth, like a fish drowning in the air. Her blue-gray eyes darted, never landing on the young woman beside her—the young woman who looked so little like her, whose colors were dark, like her father's, whose lips were full and soft and whose tall frame already showed so much more strength and poise.

Aurelie watched and waited for the word hovering on those lips. She wanted to tell her mother that, whatever was happening, they could face it together, that Aurelie was ready to help, if only the queen would let her. But the words stuck in her throat. *My name, that's all*, Aurelie wished. *Just say my name.*

Queen Yolande released a ragged breath. "Follow me, Child," she said. Then she turned and strode jerkily down the corridor.

"Yes, Maman," Aurelie said. She glanced back, catching one of the guards ogling the loose, braided tangle of her black hair, and she hurried to follow, sweeping her locks forward over one shoulder.

She had to swallow down another gulp of fear with the enormous unfamiliarity of the place. They were in a narrow, unlighted corridor with a turn at the end, and the guards walked behind them so that Aurelie's shadow stretched before her, and every step she took fell into darkness—darkness that expanded in her mind like the maw of a great, long dragon. But they turned the corner, and there was no snaking tongue nor glinting teeth, only another corridor with doors.

Aurelie tried to move gracefully, as though she were at ease, striding with her mother through their castle, but her eyes flitted back and forth, hoping they weren't watched or followed, counting doorways and turns so that she could remember the way back to her tower. They moved through a series of small passageways and came to a large open door. Aurelie teetered on the edge of it, shocked by the vastness of the place beyond. It was not even a room but another hallway, with more doors and openings, yet it was wider than her tower, her world, and it stretched as far as some of the city lanes she could see from her window.

The blood rushed to Aurelie's face, and she felt the dizzying sense that the rules of the world were changing faster than she could take in and that she would lose her balance and fall. But the cold, soft touch of Yolande's fingers wormed into her own, stronger hand, and she steadied, focusing on another, worse dread: that she would crush the queen with slightly too firm a touch, with just a little too much love or need. And so Aurelie moved forward again, trying to match the light pressure of the queen's hand and imitate the restrained step, focusing on her mother's vulnerability so that she would not have to think about her own.

Torches burned from wall casings in this hallway, emitting the faint heat of neglected glory. Aurelie scanned the fraying banners and smoke-stained crests declaring the noble families of the Free Country and the ranks of knights at the king's disposal. A vast door opened to the left, revealing a glimpse of a much larger space, a great hall, streaked with moonlight from tall windows. The king's own crest, a silver eagle in a crimson sky, hung across from the opening. Aurelie observed it all at once: the hall on the left, much too big and empty, and the king's banner on the right, much too ragged and stained and hidden. She felt the prick of guilt for her quick judgments, and she tried to focus on the path ahead.

They were turning into another small passageway, and against her sense of duty, Aurelie was slowing down, preparing to beg the queen to stop and explain where they were going and why. Then Queen Yolande herself halted and held up a hand.

Aurelie could hear the thumping beat of her own heart, and she took a shuddering breath. Reddish light came from somewhere beyond the turn of this passage, and in that place, faintly, someone was uttering a strange whining moan. Aurelie's nose tickled with the smells of flesh and rot.

The guards shifted, and one coughed, but Queen Yolande walked slowly forward around the turn of the passage, and Aurelie followed. A blast of heat hit her face, and in the span of a breath, Aurelie took in three massive fires, bubbling cauldrons, empty spits and rows of gleaming knives.

Then the quiet moaning erupted into shrill, inhuman screams.

Queen Yolande shrank back, and the guards ran forward, swords raised. Aurelie's view was momentarily blocked, and she heard the screaming escalate into a crazed yowl, punctuated by bodies slamming against each other and a loud smack of something hard hitting something soft. A piteous wail burst out, and a deep voice entered the fray, cursing harshly.

Aurelie's thoughts raced: Her moment of reckoning had come at last. The queen had struck a bargain with the Devil. They were standing at the gates of Hell, ready to feed him a human sacrifice, and somehow it was Aurelie's duty to slake his wrath in order to save everyone else. Perhaps she could try to run away now, while the others were distracted, but a nobler impulse, or maybe just guilt, stayed her feet. She could not escape without leaving the queen, her mother, stranded at the abyss.

"Non adversus carnem!" Aurelie shouted, and she pushed past Yolande and ran into the room toward the flames.

A vast, sweaty woman loomed, backlit by the blaze, and raised a broom high over her head.

Is the Devil a woman? Aurelie wondered. Then she scrambled back until she felt the brush of the queen's robes behind her.

The great woman turned and lurched toward them. She charged, and Aurelie closed her eyes, wanting to duck or run away but instead simply flinging out her arms, her body protecting the queen and one hand still clutching the pitiful shield of a book. The broom crashed down and hit with a hard smack against the floor. Two cats, yowling and scratching, rolled by, just out of reach, and raced past the queen and out of the room.

"Damn beasties," the large woman muttered, recovering her balance and tossing the broom against the wall with a clatter.

Aurelie released her breath and shuddered.

The woman stooped and picked up a bloody mouse, sniffed it and, without looking, threw it behind her onto a cutting board. Then she turned toward the queen and bowed. "It is prepared, your Majesty."

Queen Yolande stood frozen, lips pressed together, a muscle twitching in her cheek. The guards were chuckling and wiping sweat off their faces. One pantomimed the hissing fear of the cats. Aurelie looked around, taking in the large woman and the room. At last, comprehension dawned: This was not Hell but a kitchen. Aurelie let out a peel of nervous laughter and covered her mouth with her hands.

"Enough," Queen Yolande said with a tight wave of her hand.

She looked angry, and Aurelie kicked herself inside, remembering that she had pushed the queen aside in order to enter the room. *Foolish, delusional princess.* She should have let the queen take the lead. The queen was the one who understood what was happening and what to do next. Aurelie's only duty was to obey.

The guards, too, quieted instantly, snapping to attention.

With another wave from the queen, they stepped back, swords raised. One took position guarding the entryway. The other received a key from the queen and locked a smaller, wooden door, then moved to another wide opening and struck a defensive stance.

Aurelie studied them. This place might be only a kitchen, but even so, this rendezvous did not feel like an innocent excursion for a midnight snack. More than ever, she wondered if they'd come here for some noble purpose, or if they'd chosen this meeting place to deliver her to that terror who lurked in the shadows of her story, the one so hungry to pierce her flesh and take possession of her soul. Again, Aurelie scanned the bubbling pots, the hanging knives, and now, blocking every exit, a naked sword glinting red in the firelight. The big woman, the cook, presumably, took a boiling pot and poured it into an enormous, human-sized cauldron sitting on the floor before the fire.

"What are you waiting for, Mathilde?" Queen Yolande said. "Let's finish this."

Aurelie glanced back at the queen, and in that moment the rough, sweaty hands of the cook closed around her waist and removed her belt, then began to pull at her dress. A wave of terror overcame Aurelie's wish to remain dutiful, and she slapped back the woman's hands. They might have been stronger than her own, but Aurelie was propelled by the will to live, and the cook drew back, cursing.

Queen Yolande released a hiss, barely audible. Everyone in the room stopped and turned toward her. "Look away," she said to the guards, who were staring, jaws slack. Queen Yolande turned toward Aurelie. "It will be over more quickly if you don't struggle," she said, and she smiled.

That smile cut through Aurelie's heart and her will to resist. She choked back a sob and let her arms go limp. She thought of Sera and wished now that she had at least said goodbye. Mathilde, unpracticed and angry, took hold of Aurelie's dress and chemise and pulled them off, tearing the neckline of her tunic, and then yanking off the undershirt. Aurelie's cheeks burned, and she wondered for a frantic moment whether she should try to cover her breasts or her womanhood, but she did neither. She was a princess, after all. She felt the warm draft of the fires against her bare skin, and she felt the energy of a room full of people, all gathered to enact some purpose, some higher will, upon her, their princess. She lifted her chin, not deigning to look around at any of them but preparing herself to meet her fate. The cook placed a stepladder in front of the great cauldron, and Aurelie climbed, watching its dark water flickering with the reflection of flames. Was this the queen's way of saving her from the curse, from that other more damning fate? Aurelie regretted leaving the tower. She regretted not fighting harder to live. And now it was too late. She stopped at the top of the ladder and told herself to maintain dignity, to play out her role. But oh, she did not want to die.

"Indecent," Mathilde muttered. Then she shoved Aurelie into the pot.

Scalding water engulfed Aurelie. Suffocating heat pressed against her eyes, ears and nose. She opened her mouth to scream, and it filled with water, choking and burning her throat and lungs. The moment of that first shock split and fractured into an endless sensation of time and space in which she felt trapped and suspended, hair lifting, limbs thrashing but finding no purchase, lungs drinking only treacherous water. And then she thrust her head above the surface, heaving and gasping, and she realized that she was not dead. She was not even dying. She was getting a bath.

Aurelie brushed the water out of her eyes and forced the air to flow in and out of her lungs and grow steady. She gritted her teeth and fought back the urge to both laugh and cry. This horrible pageant was not a human sacrifice after all. It was only a bath, that thing that other young women did on the eve of special occasions, such as the name day of their sixteenth year—the day that Aurelie was supposed to meet her people for the first time, and the day that she was supposed to die. But Aurelie did not feel any more cleansed or prepared in that moment. She felt like the brunt of a harsh joke.

Queen Yolande stepped forward and dropped some bitter smelling herbs into the bath. She made the sign of the cross. Aurelie looked up, her cheeks flushed and brown eyes burning. The queen saw the look, and her own blue-gray eyes widened. Her hand, still outstretched, trembled. Her face took on a half-pleading, half-vindictive look. "You needed to cleanse yourself, Child," she said. "There's no reason to stink."

"Why?" Aurelie whispered. "Why don't you ever just call me by my name?"

A tremor passed through Queen Yolande's body, and she took a few steps back. Then she knelt and began uttering a low and unintelligible prayer.

Aurelie released a breath and tilted forward, locks of thick, black hair falling around her face. She sank a little deeper into the bath, her dark skin blending into the darker ripples of water. Despite her internal anguish, the hot water soothed her, sent pleasurable tingles across her flesh and forced her muscles to relax. Queen Yolande was still muttering her prayer, and Mathilde was rubbing forcefully into Aurelie's shoulders and back. The guards might have been sneaking looks. But Aurelie felt alone. She let go of the pressure to show something, to be something—to be a princess—and she eased into the forgiving water and cried.

Afterward, the strange cook rubbed Aurelie dry and gave her a stiff, new undershirt and chemise—stitches unknown—to put on underneath her old, now torn tunic. Then, while the queen looked on, Mathilde began a new kind of torture, yanking a wooden comb through Aurelie's wet curls. When she finished, Mathilde tied it all into long, tight braids that she wove in a ring around Aurelie's head, like the tonsured hair of a monk. Aurelie looked up at her mother, whose own hair Aurelie had never seen. "Tighter," the queen whispered. Then the small party retraced its shadowed passage. This time Aurelie felt less fear, and she noticed that the queen's hands shook and that she had instructed the guards to keep their weapons unsheathed.

As they reached the old tower stair, an overwhelming sense of weariness washed over Aurelie, and she shuddered. She had not been bargained away to the Devil, not yet. But she had not escaped him either. She was returning to the home that also served as her prison, and she was unexpectedly glad to be back. Yet she still knew that there, in less than a day, her fate would be decided forever. By sunset tomorrow, she would either leave the tower for good or end her waking life inside of it. At the top of the stair, she waited for the queen's shaking hands to fit her key into the lock, turn it and step away. Then Aurelie pushed open the door.

A wrinkled face, wild with rage and fear, stared out from the dark. Aurelie drew in a sharp breath, stepped forward and collapsed into the warm, familiar embrace. It was Sera, strained with worry, smelling of herbs and peat smoke and human. And there, in the bosom of the woman who was more her mother than her mother, Aurelie finally felt safe.

The lock clicked behind her.

Sera held on, not letting Aurelie go till she'd explained that the journey involved nothing more harmful than a forced bath and a terrible hairdo. Then the old woman patted the keyhole and muttered a few choice words to the door and sighed. She went over to the hearth and stoked the fire with another peat log. Then she wandered around the room, continuing to mumble angrily, stopping occasionally to shake her finger and utter warnings about the dangers of sending a young woman to bed with wet hair.

Aurelie could not bring herself to undress. She lay stiffly on the fur-lined bed, her blanket of yellow wool pulled up to her chin, her eyes open, studying the tall stained-glass window. The painted panes showed images of smiling saints—her friends since early childhood—and nearly every one of them was suffering a brutal death. Marguerite, who was stepping out of the belly of a dragon, gazed up toward Heaven with a beatific smile. And for the first time, Aurelie wondered if that smile was false.

After a long, weary spate of muttering, Sera climbed into bed, wrapped her arm around Aurelie's waist and fell into a restless, twitching slumber. But Aurelie stared up at the dark rafters of the tower overhead, her constant ceiling for as long as she could remember, and she could not sleep. She closed her eyes, but her mind kept replaying the night's events. She had felt so terrified, so sure she was being betrayed and surrendered to her enemy at last. She had reckoned with death and damnation. And then her fears had turned into nothing. A delusion. A bath. But she felt no release, no catharsis.

Her mind went over her observations again: the forced march, the blocked exits, the queen's crazed look and, worst of all, the risk of leaving the tower on the very day of her curse.

It was only a bath, Aurelie told herself. But logic and the survival instincts of a woman who had so far survived a life-long curse would not let her rest with that conclusion. A bath could have been arranged more safely and easily, with a basin and a towel, inside the tower room. No, this wasn't about cleansing. And it definitely was not about making her feel more prepared to meet the world outside. So, if it wasn't about either of those things, Aurelie wondered, then what was it about? And the more she tried to evade the idea, the more it chased her and threatened to topple her and swallow her whole—until she finally seized the thought and looked it full in the face.

And then she recognized that the bath did look like a rite or a ritual of some sort. But not for a beloved daughter. Not for a party.

It looked like the prelude to a human sacrifice.

2

Stained Glass

Trumpets blasted through the stillness of the morning, tooting the lilting notes of a gavotte. Aurelie woke, wincing. She'd heard the herald's new apprentice practicing for weeks, and she'd thought it charming at first, but the loud volume of this public performance did not improve his skill. "Whose idea was the gavotte?" she said, kneading her throbbing head.

"All I know is they didn't ask us," Sera said. The old woman, draped in her loose brown dress, stood on the deep sill of the window, peering out of the singular clear pane in the center of the colorful glass. She might have looked like a statue in a church if she had not been hunched and facing in the wrong direction.

"Last night—" Aurelie began. Dark memories teetered on the edges of her consciousness.

"Try not to worry about it, mon caneton," Sera said. "It's not our problem your mother's a witch." She beckoned. "Come look."

Aurelie rolled out of bed, adjusted her stiff new undergarments and stepped up beside Sera.

Below her window, the courtyard was filling with a party of nobles, riding, strolling and rolling in on banner-bedecked wagons. Aurelie studied the men—any one of whom might be a prospective suitor. She noticed that fashion had shortened their tunics since the last gathering. A few of them wore little more than tight stockings over their long legs, yet their shoes looked too large, some of them twice the length of a regular foot. Aurelie had to laugh. They all looked so completely unfit for anything but dancing. The women had dressed for show, too, their gem-colored dresses trailing such long sleeves and trains that they had to be tied up. But what stood out was their hair. They wore it loose, flowing out in shiny ringlets and waves, and the few who wore veils or nets had designed them both to hide and to reveal, a calculated peek-a-boo of feminine sensuality. Aurelie groaned with wonder—and worry. She hoped that she, too, would have a dress like theirs. She hoped that her extravagant father and even her proud mother would want that. Aurelie reached up and touched the coil of hair wrapping severely around her skull. *Tighter.* The queen's whisper flashed through her mind, but she pushed it away.

A playful wind blew just then across the party of nobles, displacing veils and scattering hats, and in that moment, the most noble members of society all began to squawk and flutter like a nye of pheasants. Aurelie let out a hearty laugh.

One man riding a black palfrey laughed too as he broke apart from the floundering group. He waved away a footman offering a stepladder and shook off another one trying to take his reins. Then he leapt down from his horse with ease. He put an arm around the steed's neck, rubbed her head and spoke into her ear. The man wore no sword, and his clothes looked plain, just a green tunic and brown breeches, but they were cut well to his powerful form. Though Aurelie had never met him before, she thought she recognized the curly black hair, the sundrenched skin and the sure stance of her father's good friend, Sir Roland. He spoke a word to his horse, then turned, and she followed him toward the stables. Just before he passed out of sight, he looked up.

Aurelie pulled away, heart beating fast. Then she put her hands over her flushed face and laughed at herself. Tower life had made her shy, but she did not intend to stay that way. She grimaced at Sera, who had stepped out of view as well, and then she covered the new tear in the neckline of her dress with her hands, and she looked back out of the window.

The man was gone.

Aurelie gazed down at the others, tumbling off their horses and into their servants' arms, and she smiled. Tonight she would be dancing among this whole merry group. More than that, she would be introduced as their future queen. She would have the honor of guiding and leading all these people—both the ridiculous and the admirable. She felt a swell of love and gratitude at the glorious weight of her destiny. By comparison, the challenges and restrictions of her life in this moment seemed small.

"They are all here for you, mon poussin," Sera said, elbowing her in the ribs. The old woman had a face much like the sun-deprived color of a parsnip, and when she smiled it scrunched into a myriad of wrinkles.

Aurelie grinned. "That's a lot of good-looking men just for me."

"Oh, I doubt many of them are good enough for you," Sera said. "Your father wouldn't settle for less than a duke, I'm sure."

"Or maybe a prince," Aurelie said.

"You think you can lure one of those into the Free Country?" Sera said.

"Why not?" Aurelie said, winking. "Maybe my legendary kindness or beauty will draw them in."

"Only if your legend doesn't scare them away," Sera said, frowning. Her frown produced almost as many wrinkles as her smile.

Aurelie fell silent, still gazing out. She did not want anything to steal the joy she felt this morning.

Sera clambered down from the sill. "Anyway, don't worry," she said, patting Aurelie's rump. "They all come with the same goods."

Aurelie grinned and tried to laugh, but it sounded forced. The sudden urge came over her to sit down and count all the stitches in her new chemise, but instead, she pressed her forehead against the cool glass, and she searched the view. Every morning, she looked out of this window, checking in on the people she loved, and she would not abandon them today. Down the slope of the castle hill, the King's City rose with its majestic cathedral and broad city square, surrounded by winding cobbled streets, shops and houses. The river Doubs wrapped all around the city, like a bright shield, and on the far side of it, the king's wealth grew in the fields and vineyards that stretched across the valley and into the hills. Aurelie held her breath, sensing that the normal rhythms of the day were off. The streets looked empty, and only guards stood about in the main square and on the bridges. Even the peasants were keeping away from their laden strips of the fields. Were they so afraid of this day too?

Sera tapped Aurelie's leg and held up a hunk of bread. "Hungry?"

Aurelie shook her head. "I'm fine. You eat. But I would like some—" Her voice trailed off before she spoke the word. *Water.* She sank down onto the windowsill, pulled at the new chemise to stop it from chafing and wrapped her arms around her knees. Flashes of memory from the night before came back. The sudden pressure of water against her face. The burning lack of air in her nose and throat. A scream that was never heard. Aurelie closed her eyes and gripped her head and told herself to remain calm. But the trumpeting fanfare outside made an undanceable, jarring music. Aurelie yanked at the braided coil, trying to relieve the pressure, but she could not untie the long, continuous knot.

The church bell tolled, one, two, three—noon. Aurelie released a shuddering breath and smiled. Nine hours left till sunset. Only nine hours left for the Devil to try to come and collect her soul.

The door at the base of the tower scraped, and Aurelie jumped. She rose and moved softly to her own door, listening for the footstep. Only three people had a key into her room. Two of them could not open the door alone, without Aurelie's key inserted into the other side of the lock. It was a perfect system. Aurelie heard the king's light, quick step, and she relaxed. She noticed Sera was tucking a long strand of graying-brown hair back into her knotted wimple and retreating with the chess set to the hearth, so she must have had heard it too. Aurelie slid her key into the lock, waiting.

"Cuckoo!" King Hugh called from the landing.

Aurelie turned her key just as he turned his, and she threw open the door. "Bonjour Papa!"

"Bonjour ma chère!" King Hugh said. "Bonjour Madame Sera!" He stooped to enter the room with a flow of silver robes, trimmed in red. He handed off a round platter of food to Sera, and then he picked up Aurelie and spun.

Aurelie laughed, kissing his cheeks, which were the same deep brown color as the royal eagles that flew down from the heights. Aurelie pressed her own cheek into his prickly black beard, and she felt the dampness of recent tears. "What's wrong, Papa?" she said, pulling back.

"Nothing," King Hugh said, putting her down and swiping a silky sleeve across his eyes.

"Are the nobles giving you trouble?" Aurelie said, tilting her head.

"Unbearable," King Hugh said. "One of them asked me what kind of grass I feed the horses. As if I would know!"

"You should have told them it's grass chosen by unicorns and blessed by the pope," Aurelie said, grinning.

"Exactly," King Hugh said, snapping his fingers. "Next time you will tell them for me."

"And you water it daily under your own toilet," Aurelie said.

King Hugh bellowed with laughter, doubling over and letting the tension shake out of his tall, wiry frame. He straightened, wiping his brown eyes, and pulled the thin gold circlet off his head and tossed it on the bed. "Tell me, ma rose," he said, gesturing. "What is this disaster that has be-fallen your hair?"

Aurelie made a face. "Mother did it," she said.

"That woman," Hugh said, shaking his head. His own sleek hair fell in perfect spirals to his shoulders. He sat on the windowsill and pointed to the floor. "Sit. I will fix this myself."

"You?" Aurelie said, glancing at Sera, who was absorbed in her own game of chess.

The king raised an eyebrow.

"All right," Aurelie said, shrugging and sliding to the floor at his feet.

Hugh ran his hands over the coiling braids, finding a loose end and wriggling it free. Aurelie closed her eyes, appreciating the gentle tugging against the awful tension of the coil. Hugh's fingers moved deftly, easing free a lock of hair, then smoothing it between thumb and forefinger before moving on to release another. Then the movement of his fingers stopped, and he let out a sigh. His hands dropped to his lap. Aurelie craned to look up. Her father's shoulders looked slumped, and his face had gone slack. She touched the braids, still mostly coiled around her head, and she moved to sit beside him.

Hugh put his arm across her shoulders. "I suppose you had better get Sera to do it," he said. "I forgot how much patience it takes to undo a woman's hair." He forced a smile. "Tell me, ma chère. What would you like to do first when you finally leave the tower?"

Aurelie stiffened as disturbing memories flooded back into her mind. She had already left the tower. She had been taken to a flaming kitchen that served up dead mice, and there a strange woman had torn off her clothes and plunged her into an unholy baptism. Aurelie frowned, trying to remember what question her father had asked.

"I was about your age when I first killed a person," Hugh said.

"What?" Aurelie said, turning to gape at him. Her father said nothing. His eyes studied the closed door of the tower, though his mind seemed somewhere else far away. Aurelie watched him, and she noticed in that moment that, for all his years of ruling, his face did not have even one single wrinkle.

"He was one of those traitors from the Duchy—damn them," Hugh said. "One of the nobles who left with my half-brother, the so-called prince. Anyway, he challenged me to a duel, insisted that I defend my right to rule the Free Country. Other nobles were threatening to turn against me at that point, and the mountains were already stained red with my people's blood." Hugh shook his head. "I had to end it. So I ran him through the throat with my sword." Aurelie watched her father's hands, fingers twirling, while the rest of his body held perfectly still. "I killed other men after that," Hugh said, "but I still remember that day. How I felt. I threw up after. But that's not important. What's important is that I'm still king of the Free Country."

Aurelie nodded.

Hugh looked at her. "You have it in your power to be the most beautiful flower of them all tonight," he said. "If that's what you wish, then I don't want anything to hold you back. Not your hair. Not anything—not anyone—else. Understand?"

Aurelie nodded again though she felt confused. She wanted to say something fitting, but only one thing came to mind. "Mother took me out of the tower last night."

Hugh's body went rigid. "She what?"

"She took me to the kitchens for a bath," Aurelie said. "And for this." She gestured to her hair.

Hugh surged to his feet, silver robes swirling around his knees. "That woman! That madwoman! I will—I will not let her—"

"Wait!" Aurelie said, jumping up and grabbing his arm. "It doesn't matter now. I'm fine. I'd rather you stayed with me."

King Hugh lurched, swaying, regaining his balance. He ran a hand over his face and hair. "You are right. We must put this out of our minds, ma chère," he said. "We must focus on what's most important for you."

Aurelie met his eyes. "Most important for me?"

Hugh gave a rueful smile. "The party tonight, of course." He held out his hand. "Will you honor me with this dance?"

Aurelie hesitated a moment, then smiled back and reached for her father's hand. He hummed softly as they swept across the room, skirted around the bed and did a turn-step at the wall. Hugh supported her fingers delicately in his, guiding their dance steps with precise impulses of his hand. Her own hand responded with just the right balance of engagement and resistance, as if the connection of their hands was its own kind of dance. The movements, so familiar, soothed Aurelie's spirit and reminded her that in some ways, she was very well prepared for the next stage of her destiny. She was prepared, at least, to meet the world outside—one practiced dance-step at a time.

"Now, I don't want you to feel nervous at the dance tonight," Hugh said, still tapping his foot and guiding her along to the beat. "Maybe I didn't teach you all the steps, you know, or maybe someone there could make you feel a little uncomfortable." Hugh chewed on his lower lip. Aurelie circled him in a slow promenade, and her eyes sparkled, amused to see her father, the king, looking so nervous. Hugh broke into a grin. "All I'm trying to say," he said, "is that you are ready. If you get lost in the dance, just stop and show off how lovely you are." He struck a pose, holding out an imaginary skirt and batting his eyelashes.

Aurelie laughed and pushed away. She was afraid of eternal damnation. She was afraid of leading her country poorly. She was not afraid of a dance. She closed her eyes and hummed, changing the tune, allowing it to thrum deeply in her throat. She didn't try to fit her imagination inside of that cold, stone great hall. Rather, she opened herself to an image of the moon shining over a hill, where she'd seen peasants lighting bonfires and their dark forms dancing around the flames. The Free People always lit fires on feast days, and Aurelie always watched them. Though she could not make out their steps from so far away, she understood their energy, their passion. She spun, feet stomping to a rhythm. Her hips swayed, and her hands rose toward the stars. She breathed in, imagining the scent of a thousand logs burning at once. Her body warmed, finding the movement of slow crackling flames. She pressed her closed eyelids together and saw sparks rising into the sky.

When Aurelie opened her eyes, Hugh was staring at her with his mouth open. "Like that," he said. "Dance like that, ma chère, half-fairy daughter, and no one will see anyone else in the room."

Aurelie gave a bow to hide her blush.

Hugh swiped a hand across his eyes, rubbing forcefully. "So many years," he said, "and I can still learn something new about you." He exhaled sharply. "I—I want to give you a gift, a reward for all your years of—er—time spent in this place, something nice that you can think about if there is ever an unpleasant moment in the midst of this long day. What would you like?"

Aurelie did not answer. She was surprised by the words, by the question.

"I suppose you don't need any more books," Hugh said. "Anyway, you have taken all of mine. Dresses? Of course, you shall have dresses. Jewels?"

Aurelie frowned, considering.

From her place by the fire, Sera muttered, "Always say yes when a man offers you jewels."

Hugh laughed, then groaned ruefully. "How I wish that I could decorate you with all the gold and jewels of one of the princesses of Zagwe!" he said. "Nothing less could match your beauty." He shook his head. "But you will find more jewels in the treasury of that church down the hill than you will find in the storerooms of our poor little French kingdom."

"I don't need jewels to help me get through the day," Aurelie said.

Sera clicked her tongue.

"Of course, you don't," Hugh said, putting an arm around her shoulder. "You are wiser than our Bishop Aimery in that way." He sighed. "Still, I wish I could share with you some of those glories of my youth—the churches in Lalibela, cut from just a single slab of stone! And the bibles—penned with all the radiance of Ethiopia! How pitifully Bishop Aimery would view his hoard of Frankish penance if only he could see the wonders, the devotion and the mastery of those monks of Begwena."

Hugh squeezed Aurelie's shoulders. "Yet we do have our own kind of wealth here, ma chère." He pointed toward the stained-glass window. "It is the Jura, wild and free. It is our people, the Free People, with spirits to match their mountains. We might only be a small kingdom with too few jewels to adorn our daughters, but we have the Free Country—we are the Free Country!"

Aurelie followed the line of his pointing finger, and she felt stirred by her father's words, but at the same time, her breath had begun to feel shallow and her head light. The stained-glass window, for all its beauty, obscured the view. From where she stood, the only thing visible through the clear pane of glass was the pale blue sky.

Hugh snapped his fingers. "That's it! I shall take you on a trip around our kingdom once all this is over. What do you think? How is that for a king's present?"

Aurelie smiled and tried to answer, but the words stuck in her throat. She swallowed and tried to nod, but she felt immobilized. She could not bring herself to accept her father's wonderful offer.

Hugh peered at her. His brow furrowed. "I have missed the mark," he said. "You wanted something else, didn't you? What is it? Tell me!"

Aurelie released a tight breath. "There is something," she said. It hurt, somehow, to speak her true wish out loud.

"Yes, yes," Hugh said. "What is it?"

Aurelie felt the impulse to huddle on the windowsill and count stitches, but she kept her feet grounded. She kept her arms, her heart and her eyes open. "Will you just stay with me today?" she said. "Until sunset?"

Hugh took a step back. "That's what you want for a present?"

Aurelie nodded.

Hugh turned away. "Your greatest desire is to spend a day with your father?" He chuckled.

Aurelie watched him and waited.

Hugh scratched his head. "What if I need to use the—?" He nodded toward the covered clay chamber pot, half-hidden behind the bed.

Aurelie dropped her eyes. "Never mind," she said. "You don't have to stay."

"Wait," Hugh said, turning back. "I sense something else behind your request. Tell me, Daughter—are you afraid?"

Aurelie did not answer.

"Because you have nothing to fear," Hugh said, spreading his hands. "I took care of everything long ago."

Aurelie trembled slightly, but she looked King Hugh in the eyes. "If that is true," she said, "then why am I still in the tower?"

Hugh stared at her. He did not move. Then he glanced around the room, as if taking it all in for the first time, and his fingers began to twirl. He did not look back at her face. "I will stay with you," he said.

Aurelie released a sharp breath, and her legs wobbled. She felt that she must sit or fall down, and she eased slowly onto the edge of the bed. The sunlight looked so pretty coming through the stained-glass window. Hanging specks of dust caught in its light and became radiant.

"How shall we pass the time?" Hugh said, rubbing his hands together. "A game of chess, perhaps?"

Aurelie didn't answer. She twisted the yellow blanket in her hands and watched the dust motes floating lazily in the ray of sunlight.

"The chessboard, Madame Sera," Hugh said, snapping his fingers.

Sera didn't move. She clutched a rook, frozen in mid-play. "I was about to win," she said, her voice coming out like a croak.

Hugh crossed his arms. "I get more respect from the jesters."

Sera's hazel eyes narrowed into slits across her scrunched and wrinkled face. "I will bring you the chessboard," she said, "if you promise to play a fair game."

"God's blood!" Hugh said. "Are you accusing me of foul play?"

"No, your Majesty," Sera said, raising a crooked finger. "I'm accusing her." She pointed.

Hugh swiveled toward Aurelie. Aurelie flushed and shook her head.

"What's going on?" Hugh said.

"Stultus est sicut stultus facit," Sera said. "Your daughter has been playing stupid to let you win."

Hugh's mouth dropped open. "Is this true?"

Aurelie winced and shrugged.

Hugh snatched the chessboard from Sera, sending chess pieces flying. He stalked over to the bed and sat, flinging his robe back over one shoulder. He glared at Aurelie. "Then play your best today, Daughter," he said. "And may the best win."

Sera ambled over and deposited a skirt-full of chess pieces. Then she hobbled back to the food tray and crunched noisily on a chunk of jelly-drizzled pastry. Hugh set each chess piece in place, one by one, keeping his gaze fixed on Aurelie. "En garde," he said, sliding forward a white pawn.

Aurelie met his gaze. Her eyebrow crooked, and the corner of her mouth curved up. She decided then that she would enjoy playing to win—whatever the end result. She slid forward the black pawn that stood in front of her king. Hugh countered recklessly with another pawn, and Aurelie deployed the pawn blocking her white-square bishop. She watched her father's hands flutter over the pieces. Hers moved in sure, quick strokes. She slid her bishop across the white squares, cutting off the exit of her father's king. Then she slid her queen across the black squares, poised to strike. "Checkmate," Aurelie said, glancing up.

Hugh stared at the board. His eyes seemed to lose focus. He rocked forward and back, and then he made a small noise, like a moan, in the back of his throat.

"Father?" Aurelie said.

"What have I done?" Hugh whispered.

"It was just a new trick," Aurelie said. "The best swordsman—"

"No, no, no," Hugh said, stroking his hands across his hair. He reached for his crown and placed it back on his head. Then he got up and began pacing the room. "What have I done?" he said again.

Aurelie got up, tracking his steps. "It's the pawns," she said. "You have to keep them where they can protect the king."

"It's not that," King Hugh said. He turned back suddenly, searching her brown eyes. "Have I trained you so well to lose?"

Aurelie's mouth fell open.

King Hugh gripped her by the shoulders. "Listen to me," he said. "Hiding your best self is one way to survive, but it is no way to live. It is no way to thrive. My daughter, one day it will be your turn to stand up and tell the world who you are and what business you have in it, and then you must be ready."

Aurelie nodded, her heart quickening. "I am ready, Father. I am ready like you were at my age."

King Hugh let go and clutched his crown, lifting it away, rubbing at his temple. "What have I done?" he said.

Aurelie clasped his arms, and the crown fell, clattering. They ignored it. "You have done everything right, Father," she said. "You took the throne—the responsibility—given to you by your adopted father. You loved the Free Country and ruled it well. And I am like you, Father. I understand the weight of this gift, this destiny to lead the Free People. I will bring you honor today. I am your daughter—not only by blood."

King Hugh passed a hand over his face and groaned. "I know that too well," he said. He was silent for a moment, holding his hand still over his eyes. Then he turned away and added, without looking at her, "Promise me something."

"Anything," Aurelie said.

"Promise me that you will not think too badly of me once you leave the tower."

Aurelie's eyes widened.

"Don't misunderstand me," Hugh said, looking back. "I am not a bad man. I have always tried to lead my people well. I have always taken good care of you." He touched Aurelie's cheek. "Please, just promise me that you will try to look past the other things I might have done—or not done—if—when—you one day see them for yourself."

Aurelie stared at her father's wrecked face, his eyes still not meeting hers, and she understood for the first time that he needed her strength as much as she needed his. "I know it cannot be easy to carry the weight of a kingdom, Father," she said. "I will never hold your imperfections against you."

"Promise me," Hugh said.

Aurelie smiled, though her heart ached with the weight of their shared, unspoken burden. "I promise."

King Hugh nodded. "That's good," he said, clapping his hands. He strode to the window, scrutinizing the stained-glass.

Across the room, Sera started to hum a repetitive ditty.

"Sera," Hugh said, "either share something nice out of that toothless mouth of yours or keep it shut."

Sera laughed, an unoffended cackle. "I could tell you a story."

"Very well," Hugh said, "but make it a good one, nice and juicy. No moralizing today, if you please." He sat down on the bed, stretching out his legs across the yellow blanket and furs. Aurelie sat next to him, leaning her shoulder against his.

Sera rubbed her hands together, dusting off crumbs. "Once upon a time, there lived a king and a queen whose love for each other was never quite enough to produce a child."

The words—the words that sounded eerily like the beginning of her own story—sent a tickle of appreciation down the back of Aurelie's neck. She glanced at her father, whose eyebrows had furrowed, and then back at Sera, who was nibbling a bite of almond cake from the platter. "So, the story goes, the king and queen decided to ask for the help of a famous midwife," Sera said, wiping her mouth. "She was one of those hill women, a sorceress, very clever in magic and the knowledge of the earth and also very pretty. Some people used to call her a fairy. They said she was a friend of the king's, someone who had helped him keep favor with the people when those awful traitors tried to steal his throne. Some storytellers would even say that before the queen came along, the king could not keep out of this hill woman's company—or her bed."

Sera laughed, wheezing, and King Hugh drummed his fingers on the mattress. He glanced at Aurelie. Aurelie did not look back.

Sera licked her lips. "This powerful woman had stood by the king. She was loyal. She even cast spells for him. So, it was very natural for her to enter into a certain intimate arrangement with—"

"Enough!" King Hugh shouted. He rose, scattering chess pieces.

Sera jumped.

"Where did you hear these old wives' tales?" Hugh said.

Sera cowered. "People were telling the story before I came here," she said. "I don't know who started it."

"People?" King Hugh began to pace. "There is only one person who would dare spread this nonsense, this slander." He tripped over a stack of books, and his knee buckled. He caught himself, wincing, and then he looked at Aurelie, and his brown eyes widened with some internal pain.

Aurelie met his gaze, and she saw what would come next, and she accepted it.

"I must go," King Hugh said, his voice little more than a whisper.

Aurelie nodded. She felt angry with herself for believing that she could evade the curse so easily. She regretted that she'd asked for the thing she really wanted.

King Hugh released his breath like a gust of air. Then he stooped and seized several of the fallen chess pieces. "Perhaps, I will stay for just one more game of chess," he said. "I still need to win." But his hands shook as he set the pieces on the board, and they tipped and fell out of place, and he cried out and slapped the board off the bed. He clutched his head, reaching for the crown that wasn't there. "I am sorry," he whispered. "I cannot stay."

Aurelie wrapped her arms around her father and buried her face in his shoulder, drinking in his smells of soap and cardamom and cloves. This role, this duty, had always been hers, hers alone, and she knew it. "It's all right, Father," she said. "You can go."

King Hugh let out a soft moan, and he sank to the floor and pulled Aurelie onto his lap. "Ma rose," he said. "Mon petit agneau. If only I could keep you my little daughter forever."

Aurelie held him, pressing her cheek into his hair. "We will make it through this day," she said. "And we will celebrate together at the party tonight." She wiped his cheeks. Her own, hot tears fell and disappeared into his hair.

"Yes, yes, you are right, Daughter," Hugh said. "There is no reason to cry." He blew his nose on a silky sleeve, then offered it to her.

Aurelie shook her head, smiling.

Hugh smiled back and gently pushed her off his lap. Aurelie picked up the fallen crown. Hugh moved toward the door, and then he stopped and thrust a finger at Sera. "You got it wrong," he said. "The king never loved a witch. Never! He was a good king!"

Sera ducked and shielded her face.

Hugh dropped his hand and glanced back at Aurelie. "There is no such thing as a bad king," he said, and his lips twisted in a bitter smile, "because whatever a king says becomes law. That means there are only strong kings. Or weak ones." His eyes lowered. "At least, that's what someone once told me."

Aurelie held out his crown, and he took it. He reached for the door, fumbling with the key still in the lock.

Aurelie opened the door.

Hugh placed the crown back on his head. Then he walked out and closed the door.

Cool air blew across Aurelie's face, and then all was still. She waited to hear her father's key grate in the lock, but no sound came. A lump formed, dry and painful, in her throat, and she realized then that the king had forgotten to bring her a fresh pitcher of water. She closed her eyes and leaned her head against the door. She would not ask him for one. She could go a day without water. She had done it before. "Father—" she said.

"Yes, Daughter?" Hugh answered.

Tears gathered on Aurelie's lashes. "Lock the door, Father," she said.

Hugh did not answer. Then his key slid into the lock, and he turned it.

Aurelie held her breath as she listened to King Hugh's footsteps descend the thirty-three steps. She was glad that he was going away now. If the Devil really was coming to collect, then she did not want her beloved father to be in the room. Besides, she had stitches to count in her brand-new chemise.

The king's feet stepped off the last stair, and the lower tower door scraped shut.

Aurelie thrust her key into the lock and turned it.

3

Lotus in the Bog

Aurelie listened to the hard click of the lock signaling that she had kept her part in their unspoken agreement.

She had locked herself inside her own prison.

A strangled sob tore from her throat. Tears stung her eyes. She balled her hands into fists and slammed them against the door. The hard, wooden surface didn't budge, but her hand ached, a small, focused refraction of the blaze of internal pain, and another sob wrenched from deep within her guts. Her fists moved from pummeling the door to pounding and slapping against her own head and face.

"Stop it," Sera cried, leaping up.

"He's gone," Aurelie said, tearing at her coiled hair. "He left. He couldn't stay with me for even one day. No one can."

"He'll come back," Sera said, jumping to catch the younger woman's arms. "If I know anything about your father, he'll come back."

"No, no," Aurelie said, weeping. "He's not coming back, and it's my fault. I upset him. I asked too much. I always upset him."

Sera caught her arms, but Aurelie pulled free. She yanked the iron key from the lock and smashed it against her own fingers—living flesh and bone connecting with hard, unfeeling, unyielding metal. She cried out, dropping to her knees with the pain. Sera pulled the key away and shoved it into the pocket of her apron. Then she knelt and wrapped her arms around Aurelie, crumpled on the floor.

"It's all right," Sera said, stroking her hair and picking at the braid around her head. "It's not your fault. You shouldn't hurt yourself."

Aurelie shook her head, pressing her palms into her eyes. "It doesn't matter," she said. "You know the bruises don't show on my skin."

"It matters if you spill your own blood," Sera said. "It matters if the people see a tortured and broken princess tonight. You have to look your best—to be your best—for them and for your own pride. And what would the bishop say? You need to calm yourself now. You need to remember who you are."

Aurelie moaned. "I am Aurelie, Princess of the Free Country," she said. "I am Aurelie, Princess of the Free Country." She broke into a wild laugh and pushed Sera away. "Some princess I will make, half mad, unable to move more than ten paces from the tower without panicking. Even my own father says I seem part fay."

"Hush now," Sera said. "That's not important. What's important is your hair." She traced the crown of braids around Aurelie's head with her fingers. "Anyway, haven't you noticed? I am here with you. I haven't given up on you. Isn't that something?"

Aurelie took in a ragged breath. "It is," she said, "unless she comes here today. And then, mon amie, it only means that we are both doomed to annihilation."

Sera clicked her tongue. "Have a little faith," she said. "And for now, let's fix what we can. Like this hair. You have to look like a flower tonight, remember?"

The church bell tolled, and Aurelie submitted. There was nothing else to do. Sera went to work with powerful, deft fingers, finally releasing the pressure on Aurelie's brain, and Aurelie sat still, taking shuddering breaths and letting her sobs subside. The pain she felt inside remained, but the headache lessened.

After Sera finished, Aurelie's hair billowed in dry, frizzy kinks, a bit like an angry cloud of bees, and Aurelie's heart sank with the realization that she would not look well among the other noblewomen. But she wiped her eyes and pushed away the thought. She had bigger concerns today. "I shouldn't have broken like that," she said. "I need to be stronger."

"It's all the same to me, mon chou," Sera said. "It's a hard day for both of us—no matter if you want to dance or cry about it."

Aurelie moved to the fireplace and sat on that spot of the sandstone floor that had been worn smooth by so many years of sitting. She pushed a fresh peat log from the stack over into the embers and blew, watching the flames revive and slowly brighten as the peat caught. The fire released a faint, sweet scent of burning earth, and the dry heat soothed her aching face. Sera sat down beside her, on another smoothed divot, and she scratched absently at her pouchy wimple, which was knotted several times about her face. She took a bite of cheese and offered the platter to Aurelie.

Aurelie shook her head. "Why did you tell my father that version of the story?"

"What?" Sera said. Her hairless brows knit together across her forehead.

"You never told my story that way before," Aurelie said. "Why did you tell it today?"

"How do you know it was your story?" Sera said. She pushed the rest of the cheese into her mouth and poked at the fire with her foot.

Aurelie's dark brows furrowed as she stared at the bright orange flames licking the peat. "So, the story goes," she said, "that she-devil of a midwife helped the king and queen give birth to a baby girl, but afterward she resented them because she wanted more payment than they had agreed to, and so she went secretly to the christening party and cursed the baby princess to prick her finger on a spindle and fall into an endless, deathless sleep before the sun set on the name day of her sixteenth year."

Sera whistled softly. "That's one way to tell a story."

"I asked you a question," Aurelie said, looking at her.

"All right," Sera said, lifting her hands. "Fair enough. So, it was your story. Well, I was curious. I wanted to know if it was true."

"True if the king and that treacherous witch had a love affair?" Aurelie said.

Sera frowned. "True if he loved her."

Aurelie held still for a moment, her gaze turning back to the flames, the flickering dance of blue and yellow in the red. She nodded. "Did you find out?"

Sera shrugged.

Aurelie released a sharp sigh. "It's your fault he left, you know."

"What?" Sera said.

"It's your fault that my father didn't stay," Aurelie said. "Your story upset him."

"So it was my fault then," Sera said. Her hazel eyes, normally lost in a mass of frown- or smile-wrinkles, looked thoughtful. "I'm sorry."

Aurelie sighed and put her head in her hands, pressing her fingers into her skull, then letting go. "I cannot hold it against you," she said. "You are the only one who has ever kept this vigil with me."

Sera accepted the words in silence.

Aurelie reached around the fire to adjust the charred peat, to push it deeper into the hot coals. "Today I either win or lose," she said. Sera didn't answer, and Aurelie went on. "I know exactly what it looks like to win. I walk out of this tower at sunset and greet my people for the first time, and from that moment on, all the odds are stacked in my favor. I inherit a kingdom, one of the last free kingdoms of West Francia, and I will be one of the most desirable marriage partners in our country, if not beyond. I'll have my pick of suitors, and that's not pride—it's just mathematics. But I don't want to marry right away." She shook her head, cheeks glowing in the firelight. "I want rule like my great grandmother Eleanor, discovering and growing my own power until I can dazzle kings and influence politics and open the doorway of our court to art and music and science. I know we're not a wealthy kingdom. And the nobles are wily. Father already has trouble collecting his fair share of the tax. And, of course, the Duchy will always be a thorn in our side—damn them. So, I won't be wearing silks and eating chocolate every day. But it doesn't matter. The Free Country is all I've ever wanted, and it's mine." Aurelie put her face into her hands and groaned. "I have studied it my whole life. Its crops. Its trade. Its dealings with the church. I know that the mountains have kept us wild and safe. I would never try to tame or exploit this land—or trade it for any other life. All I want is to become a living and effective part of it. I want to stand in the soil that grows our food and feel the freshly tilled earth between my toes. I want to climb the heights that protect us and feel the sovereign wind ruffling my hair. I want to ride out under the banner of the silver eagle and meet my people and touch their hands and let them know me. When I have understood my country like that, I know I will be able to help it prosper. That's winning. That's what it looks like." Aurelie looked up from the flames, and her brown eyes shone with their light. She gripped Sera's arm. "I might be only an unconfident princess who has lived too long in a tower," she said, "but—God help me—when I leave this place, I will give all my heart and life to the work of leading the Free Country well."

A tremor passed through Sera, but she did not shift or respond.

Aurelie got up and began pacing the room. "Losing is harder to imagine," she said. "I understand only that the curse catches up to me. I prick my finger on a spindle, though I don't have one. Then I fall into a cursed sleep, though such a thing does not exist in any of my books of science. Then I remain in that state for eternity, beyond the reach of heaven or hell, though Father Aimery does not allow that such a thing is possible." Aurelie stopped and looked back at Sera. "I cannot understand how even one part of this evil fate could come true. So why am I so filled with dread?"

Sera poked at the fire. Her grayish hands still looked strong for her age, knobby knuckles bending and flexing. "Maybe it's just part of being a princess," she said.

Aurelie listened, waiting.

"Over in the East somewhere, there's a flower called the lotus," Sera said. Her hands moved to illustrate the words. "It's like our lily. It grows in the darkest, boggiest muck, but when it's ready to bloom, it rises above the water and opens a flower of the purest, cleanest white. At the end of the day it closes and sinks back down toward the mud, but the next day, soon as the sun's out, it opens again like nothing happened. Some say it's magic. It can clean water and heal ailments. Others say it's the womb that gave birth to a god. Some just embroider the flower onto rich people's clothing. I guess, it's an important symbol of something to everybody. But to itself, it's just a flower. A living thing. With a job to do."

Aurelie moved closer, leaning against the hearth, where the stones curved over the fireplace in an arch that had turned black with years of smoke. She looked down at Sera.

Sera's smile deepened, sending crinkles across her face. "And one day, when the bloom fades, the gardener chops it off to make room for another."

Aurelie stiffened. "Is this supposed to encourage me?"

Sera cackled, rocking back. "What encouraged them?" she said, gesturing to the saints, ecstatic and dying, on the painted window.

Aurelie glanced over her shoulder. She wasn't sure she wanted to know the answer to that question. "I don't know," she said. "God? Integrity? Maybe their belief in their cause?"

Sera's eyes narrowed. "And did they win or lose?"

Aurelie crossed her arms. "This is definitely not encouraging."

"All I'm saying," Sera said, "is that winning and losing are complicated, mon lapin, maybe more complicated than you think."

Aurelie turned and gazed again at the stained-glass window. She had read the stories of the saints over and over in Father Aimery's little book of feast days, and she knew all of them: Foi, Quitterie, Jacques, Maurice—even Georges, with his uniquely happy ending, slaying a dragon and kissing a princess. But Aurelie's favorite saint had always been Marguerite, who had been eaten by a dragon and had cut herself out of its belly with a crucifix. The image painted on the glass showed Marguerite stepping out of the torn-open guts of the beast, the train of her dress still dripping from its mouth, and she was smiling. According to legend, the saint's pagan father had abandoned her, and a would-be suitor had trapped her in prison, pressing her to renounce her faith and marry him. There, inside the prison cell, the Devil had visited her in the form of a dragon and swallowed her whole. But brave Marguerite had not accepted this first, easiest offer of death. After cutting herself out of the beast, she had endured torture with fire and then with water. Each time she challenged the crowd to witness her and called upon God for strength. Finally, her executioners silenced her forever by cutting off her head. Aurelie shuddered, mesmerized by the tale. Yet it was not the brutal torture or even the young woman's courage that kept her staring at the image on the glass. It was that one, ludicrous detail: the dragon. Why the dragon? Didn't the dragon make the whole story less believable? And weren't the other details potent enough? Aurelie wondered why the people of that time would have made up such an unnecessary fiction.

Was it just religious propaganda? Or maybe it was a delusion. Perhaps Marguerite herself had invented it, the raving figments of a broken mind, trying to process a reality too brutal to bear. Or, Aurelie thought, maybe there really was a dragon.

Far below, the lower tower door scraped, and a soft, brushing footstep swiped across the first step. Sera jumped. She wrapped her arms around the food platter and moved to sit against the wall where she would be blocked from sight when the queen opened the door.

Aurelie frowned. Her eyes scanned the room, taking in scattered chess pieces and even the tumbled stack of precious books. But she did not rush to clean up. That no longer seemed important. Outside, the wind was blowing harder. Aurelie could hear it, could almost feel it, blowing against the tower like a light but unrelenting reverberation in her own bones. She listened to each soft footstep of the queen's ascending, and she wondered what hazards those feet would bring her this time. She wondered what choices she, Aurelie, would make—and what consequences those choices would bring.

The door groaned as it opened without a knock or a second key. The queen had always reserved that power for herself, the uniquely double-headed key, and for the first time, Aurelie wondered why. She watched her mother stop on the threshold, eyes darting, inspecting, taking in the mess, taking in Aurelie's big, unbraided hair. Queen Yolande wore the same pale blue dress as the night before, and in her exhaustion, her skin had taken on the translucent purple color of fish scales. Her arms sagged under the weight of a large bundle wrapped in brown cloth. But she wore a perfectly crisp, perfectly white wimple, pulled tight across her forehead and held in place with a long, jeweled hairpin. Though she did not move to come inside, the room slowly filled with the sickly sweet smells of orange blossoms and marzipan.

Aurelie curtseyed. "Bonjour Maman."

"Bonjour Child," Queen Yolande said. "I hope you are not too weary today after your bath?"

Aurelie frowned. The disturbing memories flooded back, but she did not try to stop them this time. She let them pass through her, change her. "I am fine," she said. "How are you?"

The queen only shrugged and raised her eyebrows, studying Aurelie, and then Yolande smiled, as though they shared some special secret. "I hated to risk letting you catch a cold last night, going to bed like that with wet hair. But it seemed so much safer than taking you out to bathe during the day. More private too. Don't you agree?" The smile trembled and widened, asking.

That smile wormed through Aurelie's defenses, and she gave the expected nod. She felt sick, off balance. "I'm sorry my room is not tidy today," she said. Then she flushed, realizing that she had just called attention to the very thing she wanted to live above. She squared her shoulders.

Yolande only shrugged. "You have other things on your mind today," she said. "Anyway, I've brought you something. A present. If you want it." She held out the bundle, and her arms trembled under the weight, but she did not take a step into the room.

Aurelie moved toward her mother, but before reaching out, she glanced first at Sera, where she sat behind the door. Sera gave a slight nod. Aurelie looked back in time to see Yolande's smile twitch and flatten, but Aurelie told herself not to feel guilty, not to apologize. The queen had not earned—had even broken—her trust last night. Aurelie carefully lifted the soft, heavy bundle out of Yolande's fragile hands. Then she moved back toward the center of the room, where she could keep both women in view. She lifted a corner of the brown wrapping, and a few flower petals, dried and brown, fell to the floor. A faint, floral smell teased her senses. Aurelie pulled back the rest of the brown covering and gasped.

Inside was a cloth of scarlet red—gorgeous and costly. Yard by yard, Aurelie unfolded the material, each new layer melting to the contour of her touch, and when she held it up, she saw a gown of brilliant red, embroidered with flowers of real gold thread. The gown tightened at the waist and fell voluminous at the skirt, like a rose with too many petals.

"Red as the blood of a thousand Arabian beetles," Sera whispered, a few crumbs spewing from her mouth.

Yolande flinched.

Aurelie stared at the dress, and she couldn't speak. She had never let herself dream that she would leave the tower wearing something so luxurious, so impressive. Yet now she could see it. She could imagine herself wearing this dress. And seeing that picture in her mind, she could imagine herself becoming the worthy and capable leader that the Free Country needed. She could imagine herself moving beyond the curse of her childhood and becoming her own, new kind of legend.

"Your father gave me that dress years ago," Queen Yolande said, smoothing the keys that dangled from her belt. "It's a bit old-fashioned, edges tightening with laces like that, but it will probably go very well with your complexion, and it's a fine enough gown that I don't think you'll look amiss."

"Not even in the courts of Zagwe," Sera muttered.

Yolande pursed her lips.

Aurelie's chest heaved with emotion at this gift from her mother, at this first close-up glimpse of her dreams coming true, at this vision of her new beginning. She felt the softness of the dress against her skin, and she imagined her arm clothed in scarlet as she waved to her people for the first time. She could picture the excess yards of material twining around her legs as she danced. She felt now that if she put on the dress, she would finally be able to fully reveal, to fully embody, that glorious fire that she had always felt burning inside—that passion to live a big, beautiful, generous, unfettered and joy-filled life.

Aurelie pressed the dress against her body and moved toward the light of the window, catching rainbows in the folds of cloth. She twirled and let it wrap around her legs. She laughed and looked up, breathless, into the face of Sera.

Sera smiled back, a deep, crinkly, half-sad smile.

Yolande cleared her throat.

Aurelie's attention snapped back to the tower room, to her place and to her role—to the queen who should have received that first smile. Aurelie flushed, curtseying and murmuring thanks for the wondrous gift. But she did not look up and meet her mother's gaze.

"Well, I am glad that you seem to like it," Queen Yolande said. "Put it on, so you will be ready when we come for you. And do something about your hair. It's to your own benefit to look presentable for the world outside." She stepped back deeper onto the landing that her feet had never left. "Au revoir, Child."

Sera caught the edge of the door. "Wait, your Majesty," she said, half rising, though only the tips of her fingers appeared around the edge of the massive, wooden slab. "Don't you want to see your own daughter wearing your dress?"

Queen Yolande's blue-gray eyes deepened like pools of pain—or maybe hunger. She stared at Aurelie for what felt like the span of many heartbeats. Then she looked down at the threshold of the doorway, then back up at Aurelie, and something inside of her seemed to snap. "That is what I want more than anything else in the world," she said softly. Tears beaded on her red lashes, though they did not fall down her pale cheeks.

Aurelie's eyes widened with surprise and wonder.

Sera nodded and let go of the door.

Queen Yolande made the sign of the cross, and then she stepped across the threshold and into the room.

4

Love and Heresy

Aurelie watched her mother take one, two, three steps into the room and then stop, standing completely inside the tower room for the second time that day—for the second time in her life. Aurelie glanced at Sera. The old woman was still crouched behind the door, and she was smiling, but she gave no other sign or direction. The weight of the red dress pulled down on the Aurelie's arms, and her eyes swept the room, so empty of any other offerings from the queen. Aurelie wanted to be thankful for the chance to wear her mother's gown, for this opportunity for connection and intimacy. But instead she felt as though some small, overly protective friar were clambering up into the bell-tower of her heart and yanking on the alarm.

She glanced down, and her eyes caught on the dress, on the intricate stitches of real gold thread. One, two, three—twelve stitches to pattern a flower. Her eyes moved along the embroidered line, finding order, finding control. Thirteen, fourteen, fifteen, sixteen— As she counted, an image formed in her mind, and she saw herself on the outside, free and glorious, but her head was down, counting stitches, too afraid to look up and bless her people, too afraid to serve or lead them. And she knew then that if she ever truly wanted to leave the tower, then she must do it first inside her own heart. She crumpled the fabric in her hands and looked up.

"I am glad you are staying, Maman," Aurelie said. "Because I need you to tell me something before I put on your dress—I need you to tell me the truth."

Yolande stiffened. "The truth?"

Aurelie nodded. "Why are you giving me this dress today?" she said. Her gaze was stern, though her voice remained gentle. "Why have I never seen you wear it before?"

Queen Yolande turned away, taking a step back toward the open door. "Red is not really my color," she said, folding her arms stiffly across her waist.

Aurelie didn't speak, waiting.

Yolande glanced back and sighed. "Very well," she said. "It was made for the day of your christening. That has always been a painful memory. But I thought that bringing back the dress today would be a symbol of our triumph."

Aurelie pondered this new information, the possibility that everyone in the kingdom would recognize her gown as soon as she stepped outside, each time she waved and every time she pressed one of her citizen's hands in her own. It was undoubtedly a statement, a grim one but also a powerful one: A new queen was rising out of the punishment of the last. The cruel game had finally ended, and the board was reset. Aurelie nodded. She could be this kind of a symbol for her people—for her mother. "Thank you for telling me," she said. "I will wear it."

"Put it on, then," Queen Yolande said, gesturing limply with her wrist.

Aurelie handed the cumbersome dress to Sera and stripped off her leather belt and her torn over-tunic, tossing them on the bed. She smoothed out a few wrinkles in her new chemise, feeling all too aware of standing, once again, less-than-dressed before the queen.

Just then, the lower tower door scraped open. The stairwell echoed with male voices. Crooning voices. Singing a love song. Aurelie startled, listening. "And so, my darling, I wait for thee. My heart will not hold long, it breaks for thee—" The king's agile footsteps pattered on the stair, and they were followed by an unfamiliar thump.

Queen Yolande closed and locked the tower door.

King Hugh continued to sing in his rich bass, while the other man harmonized with a full, warm tenor. "Do not deny me thy face, thy love. Or I'll die and be naught but your angel aboooove!" Both men held out the last note, and Aurelie shivered with shock—and curiosity. The men seemed to be patting each other on the shoulders and offering congratulations, and then the king ran up the last few stairs and banged on the door. "Cuckoo, Daughter! I've brought a surprise for you."

Aurelie flushed, and she looked over at Yolande. Her mother's lips had flattened into a thin line, and she was holding up her double-headed key and staring at the door.

Sera smiled a deep, crinkly smile, and she chuckled softly to herself. Then she reached into her apron pocket and pulled out Aurelie's key.

The queen seized it and thrust it into the lock, turning it in unison with the king's.

"Wait!" Aurelie cried, wrapping her arms across her chemise as the door pushed open. "I'm dressing!"

King Hugh entered with a hand over his eyes. "I can't see you, ma rose," he said, "but I already know you're the most beautiful woman in all of West Francia."

"Papa—" Aurelie said. She glanced uneasily at the queen.

Yolande's face had darkened like a cloud bringing on a storm. She held one finger to her lips. Then she moved back against the wall, behind the open door, and Sera countered, hobbling out of her way, hunching beside Aurelie.

"It's not a compliment, Daughter," King Hugh said. "Just a fact. You must get used to such praise." Hugh swung back toward the cracked doorway, and he reached blindly through the opening, toward that other person on the landing. Aurelie caught a potent whiff of wine. "Close your eyes, man," Hugh said. "No peeking if you value your life." Then he gave a great pull, and over the threshold stepped a man.

Aurelie shrieked and grabbed the red gown from Sera, trying to cover herself.

"Bonjour mademoiselle," the man said, one hand clamped across his face. He had curly black hair, and his skin was the vibrant brown color of leaves in fall. He had rolled up the sleeves of his green tunic, and he looked younger than the king, shorter and stockier too. "It is an honor to finally meet you, your highness," he said, and he bowed.

Aurelie flushed. She had never received guests—had never been addressed as royalty—before. And she had never played hostess to a man who was not an old, blind bishop. She couldn't help but stare. And she couldn't help but smile. She saw power and training in this younger man's form as he bowed. She also noticed the faint smell of saddle and horse and sweat, and she noticed that his legs, under the tunic and breeches, looked as strong as a couple of tree trunks. She felt the heat rise to her face. "Bonjour monsieur troubadour," she said, trying to hide her smile and respectfully averting her eyes.

The man laughed. "Please, forgive our noisy intrusion," he said. Then, without warning, he broke into song again. "Laudato si, mi Signore, per sora Luna e le stelle!"

Aurelie's mouth dropped open. Then she laughed with surprise and delight.

"That is a bit of a new canticle I learned from some monk friends of mine," the man said. "I thought it might ease the awkwardness of an introduction where one is blindfolded and the other is—er—less than clothed." He bowed again.

Aurelie tried not to laugh this time—until he did. Then she let go of her embarrassment in a peel of mirth. "I only need a moment," she said. Her arms tightened around the dress, but her eyes lingered on the man, and she marveled at every detail—the muscles flexing on his sun-darkened forearm, the curl of chest hair at his open throat.

"Please, don't be too concerned about the ill timing of our visit, mes chers," King Hugh said. "More importantly, I dearly wanted two of my favorite people to meet." Even with closed eyes, the king gestured as gracefully as though he were making an introduction in court. "Daughter, this is Sir Roland. Roland, this is—" he paused, voice thickening with emotion, "—my daughter."

"Enchanté, mademoiselle," Roland said.

"Bienvenue, Sir Roland," Aurelie said. She liked that he'd shifted to the comfortable "mademoiselle."

"Are you finished dressing yet, ma chère?" King Hugh said.

"No," Aurelie said.

Roland drew in a sharp breath and took a step back.

Aurelie looked down at the massive dress, and she suddenly realized that she had no idea how to put it on. She clutched at the garment, seeking an opening, and in her haste, she accidentally dropped the whole dress on the floor. Then she tried to step in through the neck and almost tripped and fell over. She reached frantically for any way into the monstrous gown, all the while knowing that the men could hear every move and sound she made.

Sera intervened, prying the gown away from Aurelie and holding it up for her to enter from beneath. Aurelie lifted the skirt, glancing at the men. Roland stood stiffly; his expression had gone as blank as a stone. The king looked composed, even pleased. "Only a moment now," Aurelie said. Then she dove inside.

"I assure you, your highness," Roland said, speaking loudly, "it's not my usual habit to visit women's bedchambers. But, you see, your father was telling me—"

Aurelie emerged through the head and armholes of the dress and gasped for air.

Roland cleared his throat. "He was telling me—"

"I told him how you beat me at chess in four moves," King Hugh said.

"Er—yes," Roland said.

"And I told him how you like to read and quote from books in both Latin and French," Hugh said. "I told him how you're curious to know the names of every tree and flower in the Free Country."

Roland cut in. "He told me that you were distressed today because of the curse."

Everyone in the room fell silent.

Sera was tightening the laces along the sleeves and sides of Aurelie's dress with quick, sharp tugs, and Aurelie caught her breath. The words had struck her painfully, though she didn't try to understand why. She only knew that she suddenly wanted everyone to leave the room.

"I am a knight, among other things," Roland said. "And I wish to offer you my service today, lady. My protection. Perhaps you do not need it, but you deserve to feel safe as you prepare for the glory of going out to meet your people for the first time."

Aurelie held still, speechless. This stranger had burst into her room uninvited and spoken aloud of her deepest, most sacred fears and desires. Roland had seen her, somehow, though he could not see her. She watched a line of worry wrinkle across his forehead as he waited for her to respond, and she wanted to say something, to assure him, to receive him. But her mind felt incapable of fitting the cavernous needs of her heart and soul into the formalities of chivalry. And more than that, she was afraid to take this offer. She was afraid that depending on another today might somehow make her weaker—or even just a little less strong—and she needed to be strong. Yet she told her heart to grow. She urged her tongue to speak. "It's true," she said at last. "I was distressed today. I am distressed." Saying that, she felt raw, exposed.

A breath like a sigh escaped Roland's lips. "Then, lady," he said, "for the rest of this day I am yours." He bowed, holding out his hand—a gesture of offering.

On impulse, Aurelie moved forward, tugging Sera along, and placed her hand in his.

Roland started at the touch, and then he clasped her hand warmly in his own. Aurelie felt the capability of the broad, calloused palm, the power of his grip, and hope pulsed through her. Her knight would prove a fierce threat to any enemy of flesh who might try to pass through that door. Aurelie held onto Roland's hand, and she did not let go.

"I will stand by you, lady," Roland said. "I will guard your life with my own." Then he bent and pressed his lips to her hand.

The touch sent a rush of sensation through Aurelie. She noticed the softness of the man's lips, so different from the hard muscle of his palm. She noticed the wrinkle of worry easing from his forehead, a tender smile widening his lips. Roland's hand continued to clasp hers, neither of them moving to let go first. And Aurelie felt as though Roland's kiss had passed straight from her hand to her heart.

"Thank you, Sir Roland," Aurelie said, her voice softening. "I accept your kind offer with gratitude." She swallowed, surprised to find that she was swallowing back tears.

"It is my honor," Roland said, and his voice sounded softer as well. He cleared his throat. "Also, I forgive you," he said. A smile crooked up one side of his face.

"What?" Aurelie said.

"I forgive you for being the one to cause me to pick up a sword again."

Aurelie blushed. She did not know what to say.

"Well, that's excellent," King Hugh said. "Are you finished dressing now, ma chère? May we open our eyes?"

"Almost," Aurelie said, trying to regain her composure.

Roland dropped her hand and stepped away.

Sera gave a sharp tug on the gown's laces, and Aurelie gasped for breath. She glanced down and stifled the urge to gasp again. The new dress snugged tightly against every curve of her body from shoulder to hip. The neckline was cut wide, revealing the lines of her collarbone and throat, high-lighting the warm brown of her skin. Aurelie looked at Sera, and all her concern, all the vulnerability she felt about look-ing and acting like a princess, was loaded into that look. Sera gazed up at her for a moment with those hazel eyes, almost buried in the wrinkles. Then she winked. And to Aurelie, that wink said it all—it contained all the jokes, all the earthy lessons in love and wisdom, all the gruff challenges to be her-self, to seize her destiny with pride and confidence. Aurelie grinned. She squared her shoulders and shook back her hair. "All right," she said. "You can—"

"Stop," Queen Yolande said, striding into the middle of the room. "Keep your eyes closed, messieurs, and do not open them until I say so."

Aurelie winced, her heart leaping in her chest.

"God's blood!" King Hugh swore, staggering backward. He landed on a fallen chess piece and roared with pain.

Roland lowered into a hurried bow. "Your Majesty."

"Bonjour Sir Roland," Queen Yolande said. "Bonjour hus-band. What a surprise to find you two here."

King Hugh balled his hands into fists, and his eyes popped open. A dark flush spread across his high cheek bones, and he took a step toward Yolande. "Bonjour wife," he said, his voice sounding deep and strained. "I know you took her out of the tower last night. I know you risked her life for some freakish display of control."

"And what do you think you are doing now?" Queen Yolande said. "Arranging a forbidden meeting?"

"You will not pin the blame on me," King Hugh said, tak-ing another step toward her. "I'm the one who is looking out for her wellbeing."

"I gave her a bath!" Queen Yolande shouted. They were face to face. She was shaking, and she did not back up, though she had to crane her neck to meet his gaze. "Would you have presented her to the world smelling of her own filth?"

Aurelie flinched. Sera gritted her teeth.

"You never would understand a woman's needs," Queen Yolande said, looking away. "That's why I didn't ask you."

"You had no right," King Hugh said, holding up a hand close to her face, but his anger had diluted, and he merely reached back and rubbed his head, bumping against his crown. "You had no right—"

"Take a good look at her, Hugh," Queen Yolande said, gesturing with her chin.

King Hugh turned, seeing Aurelie and her new dress for the first time. The intensity drained from his face, and he blinked rapidly, staring at the gown. Then he swung away and strode to the window.

Aurelie's heart sank. She understood then that there had been some truth about this dress that she had failed to discern—or that she had not been told.

"What game are you playing?" King Hugh said. His voice sounded quiet, and he did not look back.

"This is no game, Hugh," Yolande said, taking a step toward him. "Tonight you are establishing our daughter's right to the throne."

Hugh flinched.

"This is not about protecting anyone's feelings or indulging in some personal fantasy. Remember that," Queen Yolande said. "Or do you wish to risk another contest to the throne?"

King Hugh stared at the window, breathing hard. He did not answer.

"Sir Roland," Queen Yolande said, making him jump. He started to pull his hand away from his face. "Eyes shut," Yolande said. "That's good." She took a step toward him. "You have such a noble reputation in our court, Sir Roland. I'm surprised that you would throw that away."

"What?" Roland said, stepping back. A chess piece snapped under his foot, and he groaned deep in his throat.

Inside, Aurelie groaned along with him. She did not know why or how, but she knew that the queen would weave them all into her own realm of inner torment now before scattering them again—and leaving Aurelie alone.

Not alone.

She smiled.

"Oh, don't worry about my opinion, of course!" Queen Yolande said. She took another step toward Roland. "I know your character. I know that you went on a crusade and got a special indulgence for all your sins. It doesn't matter to me what happened after that." She paused and glanced at Aurelie, then added, "I do wonder, though, how you planned to protect her now that your sword has been stripped."

Roland shifted, his jaw flexing. Aurelie saw the change in him and wondered at the words. She wished that she could alleviate his misery. Roland cleared his throat. "I am deeply sorry if my being here has offended your Majesty," he said. "The king has already offered to reinstate my sword. It was my choice to refuse that—until now."

"Such impeccable manners!" Queen Yolande said. "That was always your way." Her voice softened. "That's why I'm so confused as to why you did not consider the reputation of an unwed, undressed woman before blundering into her bedchamber and offering your services."

Roland's mouth dropped open.

"Oh, I don't wish to cause you distress," Yolande said, "but I am a mother, as well as a queen, and I formally request that you defer to my authority first before you try again to pledge yourself to a woman in my household—especially when she is not wearing clothes."

Roland flinched. Aurelie gritted her teeth.

"I didn't understand the—the full nature of the situation," Roland said. "She—her highness—didn't—"

Aurelie flushed, waiting to hear what he would say.

"Enough," King Hugh said, holding up his hand and turning back toward the others. "Are you finished humiliating my friend yet, Yolande?"

Yolande glared at him and pressed her lips together.

"Let us all be quiet now," King Hugh said. He turned toward Aurelie and gazed at her as if she were the only person in the room. A big, soft tear rolled down his cheek.

Aurelie gazed back, her eyes wide and pained. It seemed to her in that moment that her fears—and not her courage—had been justified. She had opened the doors of her heart, and it had been looted and set on fire.

Hugh walked toward her and gently took her head in his hands, and he pressed her feverish forehead to his own. Aurelie took a deep breath, and she felt her heartbeat slowly begin to steady.

King Hugh took a small bottle from his robes and uncorked it. An intoxicating fragrance filled the room, and each person who smelled it shifted or relaxed. Then Hugh raised the bottle and poured the whole contents over Aurelie's wild hair. He plunged his fingers into her locks, smoothing out the frizzy waves, restoring their shine. Aurelie closed her eyes and focused on the scent—soft, lavish and powerful all at once. King Hugh scrunched the frazzled strands of her hair, coaxing back their curl. Then he held her face in his hands and wiped the tears from her cheeks. He did not bother to wipe away his own. "I would have brought you a real rose if they did not have such sharp thorns," he said.

"I know," Aurelie whispered.

Hugh groaned, squeezing his eyes shut and lifting his face. "Hoc est filia mea dilecta," he cried out in a loud, full voice.

Aurelie's vision blurred. She recognized those words, the only words that God himself had spoken over his own son, the Christ. And she understood that her father was honoring her in the most magnificent way he knew how. She only hoped that no one else had noticed the reference. Because if they had, then she was not the only one in danger of being set on fire today.

"Mea dilecta—" King Hugh said, choking on the Latin. Then, as if to seal his folly, he translated the holy words into the common tongue: "This is my beloved daughter in whom I am well pleased!"

Hardly a breath stirred the air inside the room, but outside, the wind blew forcefully against the tower, as if seeking a way inside.

Hugh and Aurelie gazed at each other, smiling through their tears.

Queen Yolande whispered a single word into the stillness. "Heresy."

5

The Open Door

Outside, the wind picked up force, beating against the tower, and Aurelie felt that old sensation that the fortress of sandstone was beginning to shake. She looked around the room full of people, more people than she had ever met with in this place before, and she realized that every one of them had entered the room without her consent. They had found a way in, and they could leave whenever they wanted. Only she had never found a way through that door. She no longer felt that the tower was perfectly designed for her protection.

"Heresy," Queen Yolande said again.

Aurelie shuddered.

King Hugh, so tall and lithe, seemed to crumple.

"Father," Aurelie said, and she reached for him just as he took a step back. Her fingers brushed through air.

"Is everything all right?" Roland said. His arms tensed for action though his eyes remained closed.

"His Majesty the King has just invoked the words of God over a woman—a sinful woman," Queen Yolande said. "And then he dared utter them in the common tongue. No, everything is not all right."

"Please, be calm, your Majesty," Roland said. "Surely, this is a trespass of love, and God has grace for it."

"So, you claim to speak for God, too, now?" Queen Yolande said.

"We must call for his Excellency the bishop," Sera said. "He always knows what to do about heresy."

Roland jumped at the sound of an unexpected voice in the room.

"No one will speak of this to anyone," Yolande snapped. "Is that clear?" No one answered. "Sir Roland," she said. "Do I have your word?"

Roland rubbed his hand across his closed eyelids. "Will you please give me permission to open my eyes now, your Majesty?"

"Only if you promise to look at no one but me," Yolande said.

Roland let out a frustrated sigh and opened his eyes.

"Now," Queen Yolande said to him, "do you promise never to speak a single word of this entire encounter to anyone?"

A frown deepened the worry lines in Roland's face. "Yes, your Majesty," he said.

"Will you swear it by the nail-pierced hands of Christ?" Yolande said. Her blue-gray eyes glazed with intensity.

Roland's jaw clenched. "I gave you my word," he said.

"Good," Queen Yolande said. "Now, please, take my husband away before he does any more harm."

Aurelie glanced at the king, who was sitting on the windowsill and staring down at his hands, flexing his long fingers. She looked back at Roland. He had not moved. "Honor compels me to disobey," he said. "I offered my services today to the princess."

Queen Yolande snorted. "Then I release you from your promise," she said. "Now, go."

"Your Majesty," Roland said, his jaw pulsing. He looked down, collecting his thoughts, and his eyes moved over the low pallet of a bed, the fallen stack of books and the chess pieces, the bare sandstone floor and walls. Then he looked back toward the queen, and his eyes locked for a moment on her belt of many keys before looking up at her face. "I live by a code of honor," Roland said. "Whatever else you might think of me, I am a knight, and I gave my promise to a lady. She is the only person who can release me."

Queen Yolande clicked her tongue. She turned to look at Aurelie and moved slightly so that she stood between them.

Aurelie moved too, opening up her view. "Sir Roland," she said. He looked up but not at her. He stared over the king's head at the stained-glass window, and Aurelie saw that his eyes were brown as earth and that they looked too old and too sad for his young, strong body and lively voice. She wanted to take his hand again. She wanted to tell him thank you for standing by his word and staying with her, but she was struck by those mournful eyes, and the words got lost somewhere between her heart and her mouth. She pitied the man who had come to offer her a deed of chivalry and had been rewarded with shame, scandal and accusations of heresy. "Sir Roland," she said again, gently.

Roland startled and turned toward her. He raised a hand as if to shield his eyes. Yolande moved in front of him. "Lady—" Roland said. He looked up and met the icy stare of Queen Yolande.

Aurelie moved away from the queen, tried to catch Roland's gaze, but Yolande shifted with her.

"Your highness," Roland said, dropping his eyes, "Princess Aurelie, would you see fit to release me from my promise?"

Aurelie's breath caught in her throat. She held perfectly still, though inside she was reeling. She had not expected Roland to say that. She had not expected him to want to escape her prison so soon. But she should have expected it. She should never have expected anything else. Cursed women could not rely on chivalrous deeds.

Roland stared intently at the floor. "I spoke rashly, and I am ashamed," he said. "I should not have come inside your room in the first place. I did not understand the degree to which you were—unclothed."

Heat rose to Aurelie's face, and she tried to cross her arms over her chest, but she realized then that the dress had been tied too tightly to her body and that she no longer had the full freedom of her arms. Then anger blazed inside. She had not opened the door to this knight. She had not invited him in. And there were far more important matters at hand than his concern about how many layers of undergarments she happened to be wearing at the time. But she did not tell him that. Sir Roland did not ask her for the truth, and he did not deserve it. "I release you," Aurelie said, and she turned her back on him.

A hard smile tightened across Yolande's mouth, and she moved away.

Roland lifted his eyes for a brief, forbidden glance. He saw a womanly form, outlined by firelight. He saw the strength in Aurelie's stance, the unruly waves of hair. He could not see her face. "Princess?" he said softly.

"Please go," Aurelie said, trying to hide the hurt in her voice.

Roland hesitated.

"You heard her," Yolande said. "It's time for you to go. If you really want to be of use, then take my husband to his rooms and get rid of the wine so he can be sober for the ceremonies tonight."

Roland glanced at the king, who did not respond. "If the princess really faces some kind of danger today," Roland said, "then I should—"

"The princess's life is not in danger here!" Queen Yolande shouted. She winced, as if displeased with herself, then continued quietly. "Only three people have a key to this room. This whole wing of the castle is forbidden. Sharp objects, including swords, are not allowed anywhere nearby. But if you still insist on performing some kind of knightly duty, then go get yourself a sword, and I will show you where you can stand in the corridors—far enough away that you will not do any accidental damage." Yolande tapped her foot. "Do I make myself clear?"

"Yes, your Majesty," Roland said. His footsteps thumped, hastily leaving the room. The door groaned on its hinges. "I will just wait out here for the king," he called out.

No one answered.

Aurelie closed her eyes for a moment, letting the heat cool from her face, letting her heart remember its own strength. Then she turned back to the room. Her mother stood by the door, hands shaking. Sera had withdrawn to the fire. King Hugh was still sitting at the windowsill, and his gaze was turned up toward the dark ceiling above the rafters. Not a wrinkle crossed his smooth face. "Father?" Aurelie said.

King Hugh gave a hiccup. "Promises," he said. "So easy to make and so easy to break." Aurelie didn't answer. He rose, steadying himself on the wall, and then he looked at her, his gaze piercing. "But you, my daughter, will not forget your promises so easily, will you?"

"No, Father," Aurelie whispered.

Hugh nodded. "I thought so." He blinked, clearing his vision, and then he walked out of the room.

The three women stood still, listening as the men retreated down the stairs. The king stumbled twice, but Roland steadied him. The bottom door closed behind them.

Outside in the courtyard, guests were gathering, and their dull commotion carried muted into the room, but the wind had lessened. Aurelie could hear the other two women breathing softly, strained.

"Men," Queen Yolande said. "They are guaranteed power and wealth from birth, and their only task from then on is to gain more. More money. More power. More women. And more fame. They are lauded for greed and gluttony. Loved for their stupidity. And cheered on for fecklessness. If they are lucky, epic tales will be written about their noble failures. They know nothing about how to live a woman's life, nothing about the humiliation of choosing one lesser compromise over another until we become withered inside and out." She looked at Aurelie. "But it doesn't matter," she said. "They are men. And they will always swagger into our lives and tell us how we should be living better inside the tiny pumpkin shells of their own creation."

A trumpet blasted, and Queen Yolande jumped. She swiveled around, staring at the window. Muffled sounds suggested that another party of nobles was arriving and a crowd amassing. The heralds started into a somewhat more winded version of the song from earlier. "Damn that gavotte," Yolande said. She glanced around the room, and her gaze lingered on Sera, hunched by the fire. Yolande took a step back toward the open door.

Aurelie watched her mother jerk past and hesitate before the threshold of the open door, and Aurelie felt that she understood a little better now the incredible weight of wearing a queen's gown—heavy with both compromise and power. Queen Yolande had attacked everyone in the room until she had gotten exactly what she wanted. And yet, somehow, she had not won. Not really. The feeling of water pressing in on all sides flashed through Aurelie's mind, but it was the queen she saw thrashing and running out of air. Aurelie's anger fizzled, spent. "Maman," she said, "are you all right?"

Yolande flinched and looked back at her. "You probably think me a cruel mother," she said. "But you have no idea how much I've lost, how little I have left to give." She swallowed, and a soft color like the pink of a carnation bloomed across her cheeks. "At least I have never once tried to deceive you. I have always tried to prepare you for a cold, unprotected, unfeeling world outside." Yolande began to pick at a string tying a small purse to her belt. "Soon enough, you are going to feel that you have fewer options than you wished—than you expected. It is how I have felt almost all my life." Yolande stopped trying to pick at the knot and gave a quick jerk, snapping the cord. She gasped with pain. Aurelie winced. Yolande held out the purse in trembling fingers. Coins clinked. "Maybe this will make a small difference."

"Maman—" Aurelie said. There was so much she wanted to say but did not have the words to express. The thought crossed her mind that she wished she could have known

Queen Yolande as something other than her own mother. "I do not need your money," she said.

Yolande nodded. "I thought you might say that," she said. Her face looked incredibly tired, and the pink color faded from her cheeks. She studied Aurelie, her eyes moving over the young woman's face and body. Then she seemed to make a decision. She turned and held out the purse—to Sera. "Take this, for her, when she realizes she needs it."

Aurelie stepped back, surprised.

Sera nodded and came forward. She reached for the purse with an open hand, large and strong. Then, like the strike of a snake, she seized Yolande by the belt. Yolande tipped off balance and dropped the purse, silver coins rolling across the floor.

Aurelie gasped, not sure how to intervene or whom to help. Neither woman looked her way.

"What is this?" Sera said. "Blood money? A bribe? Do you really think this could make up for all your years of lack as a mother?"

Yolande did not move.

"Why don't you give her a gift more fitting for a princess, like jewels or a crown?" Sera said. "Are you so ashamed of your own progeny?" She grimaced. "Or are you just ashamed of the compromise that begot her?"

"I know what you want," Yolande said, and to Aurelie her voice sounded surprisingly unwavering and strong.

"Then why don't you give it to me?" Sera said. She took a small step forward so that the queen had to lean backward, dangling by her belt, her keys clinking and sliding out of place.

Aurelie held out her hands, reaching toward the two women, her mother and her companion, and she felt paralyzed.

"I will never give you anything," Yolande said, her teeth clenching.

"Because you have already given away everything of value that you ever had," Sera said. She pulled tighter on the belt so their bodies touched. "A long time ago."

Yolande's face twisted in rage and fear. "Take it then," she said. "And let whatever comes of it be on your hands—not mine."

Sera reached up with one hand, almost caressing Yolande's pale face. She took hold of the jeweled pin fastening the queen's wimple in place and slowly pulled it free. The starched white fabric fell to the floor, revealing the auburn gleam of Yolande's hair, tied in a thin, tight, unflattering braid, coiled around her head. A chafed red mark streaked across her forehead where the wimple had pressed into her flesh. Sera held up the pin, admiring its carved handle, ornamented with a red cross of rubies, crusted in gold. The queen kept her eyes on the pointy tip of the long, thin bone.

"That will do," Sera said. She loosened her arm, though she still kept hold of the belt, and Yolande took a step back, gasping. Sera's eyes narrowed. "I wonder, your Majesty, what kind of an indulgence it would take to pay for all of your sins?" Sera's normally close-pressed lips parted in a wide-open smile, showing a row of decayed and missing teeth. "Or," she said, "have you already given up on the fate of your eternal soul?"

Sera released the belt suddenly, and the queen stumbled back, eyes wide, nostrils flaring. "My daughter will pray for me after I'm dead," she said. "I doubt there is anyone who will do the same for you."

Sera snorted and turned her back to the queen. "It's time for you to go."

Yolande slowly backed to the door, but she stopped there. Her hands shook like dead leaves clinging to a winter tree, and her wild eyes turned on Aurelie. "Come here," Yolande said, beckoning. "Come and give your mother a kiss—my Aurelie."

The name, her name, spoken by the queen, washed over Aurelie like a tidal wave. Numbly, she walked forward, feeling Yolande's arms reaching for hers and her tight lips grazing her cheek. Then Yolande pressed something hard and cold into Aurelie's palm. "Au revoir, Child," Yolande whispered. Then she turned and fled down the stairs. She did not bother to shut or lock the door.

Aurelie stood on the threshold of the open door, breathless with shock. She blinked, staring at the empty landing, the dark staircase leading out of the tower forever. Then she looked down at the thing in her hand.

It was freedom.

It was the final say over her own life.

It was the queen's double-headed key.

Aurelie let out a long, slow breath. Then she paced a circle about the room, keeping an eye on the open door. She knew there could be danger outside. The witch who cursed her could still be out there. It might be safer to stay inside. But Aurelie also felt the swish of her dress, brushing heavily against her legs with each step. She smelled the lingering scent of roses. And much more than that, she felt a great release of joy bursting from her heart. At long last, she was free—free to make whatever choice she wanted next, free to live in her own land and among her own people. Aurelie stopped and touched the door, that thick slab of wood that she had opened so many times for others yet never once managed to open for herself. This side, the stair side, felt rougher to her touch. No little girl had spent her life leaning against it, wearing it smooth.

Aurelie laughed, turning back to Sera. "All my life I wanted her to call me by my name," she said. "Now, all of a sudden, it doesn't seem that important. Not as important as this." Aurelie held up the key.

Sera smiled, deep wrinkles scrunching across her face.

"It's over," Aurelie said. "Our terrible duty here is finished at last."

"Almost," Sera said. She cocked her head and looked down at the long, sharp pin in her hands. "Almost."

6

Tearing Away the Cocoon

A cool draft issued from the open door, and Aurelie laughed out loud again, just to feel how good it felt. The sound echoed in the stairwell. Aurelie walked onto the landing and looked down. This time she could see the first few steps of sandstone by the light of the window. The rest curved away into darkness, but the darkness did not frighten her now. She had only to walk those thirty-three steps and pass through a few corridors, and she would finally be able to feel the earth under her feet, the wind in her hair and the hands of her people touching hers. There was no choice left inside of her but to go.

Aurelie glanced back and saw Sera, watching. "Are you coming?"

Sera shrugged. "Do you want me to come with you?"

Aurelie smiled. "Of course."

"I'm not really dressed for a party," Sera said, gesturing to her faded brown garb and rope girdle. She still held the jeweled pin, spinning it absently between her fingers.

"Come," Aurelie said, beckoning. "My father promised me dresses. I will find you one. Something lovely."

Sera shuffled her feet. "No commoner can wear a lady's dress without breaking the law. Did you know that, Princess?"

Aurelie shook her head.

"It's a different world out there," Sera said. "I hope you are ready."

Aurelie smiled, a big, flushed, happy smile. "We will figure it all out once we get out there."

Sera nodded. "All right, if you think so," she said, but she still lingered.

"Don't tell me you are feeling nostalgic?" Aurelie said.

"Maybe a little," Sera said. "I suppose there's no need to clean?"

Aurelie looked around at the room, a mess of bedding and chess pieces and coins, and there in the middle, the queen's fallen wimple, and she wanted nothing more than to walk away and leave it all behind. Even the books could be retrieved by a servant later. There was no need to carry any burden, no matter how small, out of this room.

"You don't even want to count the stitches on your new dress?" Sera said, her hazel eyes dropping from Aurelie's gaze.

Aurelie frowned, studying her old companion. Then Aurelie walked back into the room and gently took Sera's fidgeting hands in her own. "Ma chère, Sera," she said, "up until this moment I have been a mad princess, trapped in a tower, and you have stood by me. I am that no longer. Now I am just me, ready to seize my destiny. Will you go with me?"

Sera moaned softly, still avoiding Aurelie's gaze.

Aurelie sighed and squeezed the sturdy, old hands between her own. "I have not forgotten that you were a captive here too, all this time. I haven't forgotten all that you sacrificed to be with me. It can be overwhelming to suddenly receive the very thing we always wanted. We can go slowly."

Sera's agitation broke. "You must at least let me fix your hair," she said, looking up and smiling.

"Of course," Aurelie said, smiling back.

Sera clapped and gave a small skip of glee. "And I would feel more comfortable closing this door."

"You can lock it too, if you want," Aurelie said, handing her the queen's key.

Aurelie turned away toward the window. She gathered her skirts to step up on the sill, then thought better of it. She might fall in the heavy new dress, or she might tear it. Instead, she rose up on tiptoes, craning to catch a glimpse of the world outside through the clear pane of glass. She could just see, far away in the hills, another party of nobles approaching. She squinted, studying the banners. Then she gasped and dropped back on her heels.

"What is it?" Sera asked.

"I thought I saw the crest of the Duchy," Aurelie said.

"Blue and yellow?" Sera said.

"I could be mistaken," Aurelie said. "They are still so far away." She frowned.

The door closed, groaning softly, and Aurelie felt it like a sigh in her bones. Sera turned the key in the lock. Aurelie had to fight herself not to run and throw it open again. "Let's finish my hair now, quickly," she said. She spread the skirt of her dress and sank onto the stone floor by the window. She could still hear the sounds of people congregating outside, and there was no terror, no military edge to their noise-making.

Sera placed the pin in her mouth, clamping it in her teeth. Then she picked up the food platter and came over and set the plate full of delicacies on the sill. With one hand, she reached down and yanked a yellow ribbon from under her brown dress. A dirty wool sock slid down around her ankle, and she kicked it off. "Never underestimate the power of a bright ribbon," she said, mumbling around the pin. Then she reached into Aurelie's hair and began parting it into plaits, carefully wrapping the strands around the long, gnarled fingers of one hand.

Aurelie relaxed at the touch. She thought about leaving the tower alone now with Sera, and she hoped that they would not get lost. She wondered if she would have to pass by Sir Roland on the way out—not that it mattered. She shifted, raising her knees and trying to wrap her arms around them, but the stiffness of the dress made it impossible.

"You should eat some food," Sera said, nudging the platter. "It's tasty."

Aurelie laughed. "I could only eat if you fed me. I can hardly move in this dress."

Sera grunted and held out an apple. Aurelie leaned forward and bit into the crisp red fruit, tangy juices running over her tongue and throat. She munched slowly, feeling a sudden ache of hunger contracting her stomach. It was the first food she'd eaten all day, and she craved more. But Sera had put down the apple and gone back to working on the hair, and Aurelie did not want to distract her. She did not want anything else to delay her exit from this tower. Besides, there was sure to be a feast waiting for her in the great hall. She smiled at the growing feeling that she was becoming the master of her own destiny.

Sera's fingers worked through Aurelie's hair, lifting strands away from the thick tresses and weaving them into intricate braids and loops that she wrapped around the rest of the hair, pulling it back to show off Aurelie's bare neck and shoulders. Sometimes, the older woman's hands shook, and she had to stop and rest. "It's a pity we couldn't get you a crown," Sera said, still mumbling around the hairpin.

"I'm sure that will be part of the ceremony tonight," Aurelie said. "Father loves a pageant."

"True," Sera said. "Anyway, I am weaving you one out of ribbon and hair. These jewels will hold it all in place."

"You are an angel," Aurelie murmured, eyes closing.

Sera only grunted, working intently, every finger holding a different strand. "So, you aren't afraid of leaving the tower?" she said.

"You have taught me to put wisdom before fear," Aurelie said, keeping her eyes closed. "I am ready to go. That's all."

Sera grunted again. Then she seemed to be holding her breath. Aurelie felt her let go with one hand, and then the long pin slid into the intricate arrangement along the back of Aurelie's scalp. Sera let go with her other hand, and the hair held in place. Sera released her breath with a whoosh. "Now, I feel better," she said, getting up.

Aurelie tried to rise but collapsed under the weight and tightness of the new dress. She held out her hands, laughing. "I am at your mercy, mon amie."

Sera raised her eyebrows. "I guess you'd better not nap today," she said. She took hold of Aurelie's hands and pulled her up.

"Never again," Aurelie said, glancing down at the low bed, its tousled yellow blanket and old furs. She moved toward the door, but Sera remained, hunkering down in her old, worn spot by the fire.

"There is one more story I must tell you before we go," Sera said.

Aurelie paused, looking back. Sera's hands, clamped over her knees, were shaking.

"This might be my last chance to tell it," Sera said. "I know, it will be hard for you to hear this. You might not even believe it. I myself am still sorting out the truth from fabrication. But after listening to the king's outburst earlier, I have more confidence in this version of the events. And it is something that you, too, must now hear and consider, mon coeur."

Aurelie touched the heavy wooden door, and every fiber of her being longed to take back that key, open the door and go out. But she stayed, listening. She was a princess, after all, and she owed Sera that much.

"So, the story goes," Sera said, "when the king and queen went to the midwife for help in getting a child, she asked for only one thing in return: a night with the king. Well, the queen must have been that desperate that she agreed, and she did not notice until later that the king did not need much persuading. So, they put the king's old lover up in a room in a far wing of the castle, and some say he spent many more than one night in her bed. After some time, the queen did swell with child, but so did the king's lover. And it was the woman of the hills who gave birth to a child first—the king's first child."

Aurelie listened, mesmerized and detached, as if this story was about people she didn't know—as if she had always known this story all along.

"The woman brought her child to the king," Sera said, "and she demanded only what was right—that he claim the child as his own and give it a name. But the queen stood against any public acknowledgment of the truth. And the king was weak. He gave in to the queen's demands." Sera's voice dropped, and Aurelie had to hold her breath in order to hear. "The king banished his lover, and he himself tore the child from her arms and ordered that it be killed."

Aurelie could hardly breathe. A cold sweat broke out on her forehead.

Sera sat quiet for a moment, absently plucking at her hairless brow. "The woman came back, of course," she said. "If she could not get her child back from the dead, then she would at least get justice. So she snuck into the christening ceremony of the queen's child, and before the babe could be named, she cursed it."

Sera shifted and glanced around the room. "You know this part of the story," she said, not looking at Aurelie. "You know what happened to that child, the queen's cursed child. But the story of the king's lover, the sorceress, goes on. The storytellers agree that the king's men dragged her out of the city and into the hills that day. They broke her body and almost broke her mind, and then they left her for dead. But, a few storytellers will add that that was their mistake—leaving her body in the hills, in the Jura. For those mountains contained the source of her power, and she drew on them as never before that day. She used her last breath to make a bargain with the gods of the hills. She bound them to keep her alive and to fulfill her curse upon the princess. Those storytellers say that the gods agreed, and they helped her survive. They say it's not only she who craves the blood of the princess now—it's the gods themselves."

Sera finished talking.

The muffled sounds of people outside grew and seemed to distort like the growling of a strange and horrible beast.

Aurelie felt faint and sick to her stomach. She wanted to sit, but she did not know if she would be able to stand back up again. "This—this story, as you call it, is almost too hard to bear," she said. Emotion cracked her voice. "It is almost impossible to believe. And yet I find myself believing. What am I to do?"

"I knew you would feel that way, mon trésor," Sera said, finally looking at Aurelie in the face. "That's why I could not tell you sooner. It was too great a burden. But now you are a woman, and you are walking into your authority. You must know all the compromises that brought you to your place of power. You must know the many sides of your story before you seize that power and choose how to wield it."

"My power?" Aurelie clenched her fists and shook her head. "The power of a princess? A woman who's lived her whole life in a tower? How can you expect me to walk out of here and wield power? How do you even know I will be able to?"

"No!" Sera said, almost shouting as she rose to her feet. "That's wrong. Even the smallest, weakest peasant out there has some kind of power, and the worst evil of all is not to recognize it and use it. The next greatest evil is to trifle it away in petty, cruel displays of control—like burning other people's books or making children and prisoners obey stupid rules. That's how most power gets pissed out of this world. But you know better, Princess. You will have great power sooner than you think. What will you do with it?"

Aurelie stared, her mouth dropped open.

Sera took a step toward her. "Some say power corrupts," she said. "But that's not true. It only reveals. It tears away the cocoon of a person and shows what was already inside—the good, the bad and the rotten."

Aurelie gasped for breath. The laces along the sides of her dress dug into her ribs and constricted the swell of her lungs. She felt dizzy.

Sera blinked, suddenly taking in Aurelie's distress, and her eyes lost their piercing glare. "What am I doing?" she said. "Heaping so many burdens on a young woman on her special day. I should stick to fixing hair."

Aurelie trembled.

Sera took Aurelie's hands and pulled her into the center of the room, coaxing her to sit. "I think that all we need do is just answer one little question together before we go," Sera said, and she sat cross-legged to face her. "I do not think it will be too hard."

Aurelie stared back, wordless. The church bell tolled dimly, but she did not count.

"You asked me to go with you out of the tower," Sera said, "and I delayed because I wasn't sure then about a decision I still have to make. You see, I would like nothing more than to go out of the tower with you now and dig my fingers into that old, neglected garden of the king's and spend the rest of my days growing herbs and helping you adjust to the world outside. But I am still bound to another duty—a promise that I made long ago and that I should fulfill as soon as my service to you has ended." Sera smiled that old, deep smile, her eyes disappearing into the mass of wrinkles. "What was it the king said about promises?"

Aurelie forced a returning smile, though her heart ached.

"I would dearly love to let the past go," Sera said, "but I am a woman of conviction. So, I suppose this is your first test of power, Princess. Would you ask me to break my vow and go with you out of the tower so we can live out this sweet little happy ending?"

Aurelie took a deep breath. So much had already been asked of her today. It was almost no surprise to give a little more. "I did not know you wanted to garden," she said, closing her eyes. "In my imagination, you would get a room near the kitchens and eat hot almond cakes right out of the oven all day long. I'd come and visit you and ask you for advice, but I'd never make you serve me." Aurelie smiled, steadying her voice. "Someday I'd take my children to visit you, and they would listen to your stories." She gazed tenderly at Sera. "I hope that all these dreams can still come true, mon amie, but for now, you must keep your word."

"I thought you'd say that," Sera said, cocking her head. "But I thought you would cry. No tears for your old Sera?"

Aurelie almost laughed, hysteria bubbling up in her voice. "How many tears must I shed today?" she said. "I am all dried up, mon amie, but I will give you what I have left." She reached for Sera, leaning forward over the great skirt till she almost collapsed into the older woman's arms. They held each other. Aurelie sighed, savoring that smell of herbs and peat smoke, and she wondered if this was the last time she would ever get to just rest in her old friend's embrace. She felt the contours of the firm, hunched body, the bony shoulders, the capable hands. "I owe so much to you, ma chère Sera," she said. "Godspeed you in fulfilling your vow."

Sera stroked her hand across Aurelie's shoulders, and Aurelie felt the braided hair at the back of her head lift and then release. A soft wisp of curl fell and brushed against her bare shoulder. She pulled back.

Sera sat upright, holding the long, bone hairpin. A look of bitter resolution glinted in her eyes. "Don't worry," she said. "It will be almost painless."

7

Mother of All

Aurelie scrambled back, trying to rise but catching her foot in her long skirt and falling. She heaved with her arms, tearing fabric and pushing back until she felt the heat of the fire behind her. She stopped, gasping for breath.

Sera sat still in the center of the room.

Aurelie glanced at the closed door to her left, then back at her companion, sitting still as a stone and holding the hairpin—a sharp, spiked object that could impale flesh. The yellowing shaft of the bone pin looked a little longer than a handbreadth, and its ruby cross sparkled in the light of the stained-glass window. Aurelie moaned.

Sera touched the pointy end of the pin to her own, pale finger, then gave a slight press. "A single drop of blood should be enough," she said. "This is a spell, not butchery."

Aurelie's head spun, and she gasped, trying to get more air.

"There's only one problem," Sera said, looking up. "This isn't really a spindle, is it?" She laughed, a light, warm sound, and she made as if to toss the thing away. Then she stopped herself. "But we could change that easily enough." She carefully pressed the pin through the fabric of her dress, across the heart. "All we have to do is make it spin thread. Then, of course, it will become a spindle—your spindle."

"No, no, no," Aurelie moaned, trying to stand up in the cumbersome dress but collapsing again.

"The mechanism of a spinning wheel is simple," Sera said. "Every part and piece works together to power the spindle, which spins and spins, causing the thread to wind into a tighter and tighter cord. Then, when the weaver sees that the thread is ready, she allows the spindle to swallow it up, wrapping the thread around and around the shaft of the spindle till it's gone, and she has to begin again. It's a wonderful design, really. Perfect dispersal of effort."

"I don't understand," Aurelie said, shaking her head. She gathered her skirt up in her hands. "You must put down that hairpin immediately, mon amie. We must leave the tower at once. And then we can get you anything you want for any purpose."

"I think you understand perfectly," Sera said. "But, just in case there is still some doubt, I will show you." Sera rose, and with her movement, Aurelie found the strength to surge to her feet. She stood, clutching her skirt, ready to spring away. Sera only walked over to the window and picked up the food platter. Aurelie countered her movement, edging along the wall toward the door. Sera took a large bite of mulberry pie, munching slowly and licking each finger, stained black with the berry juice. Then she tipped the platter, dumping the rest of the food onto the floor. "The wheel," she said, holding up the round platter. "The wheel is what spins the spindle."

"Please, stop this!" Aurelie said, her voice rising. "The stress has gotten to you, mon amie. You need to rest. Lie down. I'll go get you some water. You must be thirsty. I'm thirsty."

Sera took off her girdle of woven rope, tied it into a wide loop, then wrapped the loop around the edge of the thick platter. "A continuous cord binds the wheel to the spindle," she said, "and the spinning of the wheel causes the spindle to turn." She let the wheel dangle inside the girdle, turning it carefully in her hands.

Aurelie felt the handle of the door and pulled. It did not budge, of course. Sera had locked it. Both keys were in her apron pocket. Aurelie glanced around the room, seeing coins that could buy her nothing, crushed chess pieces that could never win her another game and fallen books that gave her no information about what she was now facing. Everything around her looked like a pathetic, woeful miscalculation of her real need. She wished now that she had simply eaten some food and asked someone to bring her some water. But it was too late. Now the only resource she had left was herself.

Aurelie took a step toward Sera. "Please, mon amie," Aurelie said. "Please, look at me."

Sera kept turning her wheel.

"Please, think about what you're doing," Aurelie said, taking another step closer. "Perhaps we are on the same side. I am learning only now that our kingdom is stained by a terrible guilt. I understand that you want justice and that you made a promise. But we don't need to use blood or curses to make this right. There are other ways. We can help each other. We are powerful, remember? Sera?"

Sera's head snapped up. "My name is not Sera."

"Of course," Aurelie said. "Let's just open the door and go outside and talk about our grievances in the light of day." Her voice caught in her throat. "I—I want to feel the sun on my face."

A small, bitter smile twisted Sera's lips. "The last part of the spinning wheel," she said, "is called the mother-of-all. That's the part that traps the spindle in place while it's being turned by the wheel and cord. But the mother-of-all can't hold the spindle too tightly, of course. No, no, no. The spindle needs at least a little freedom. It needs just enough freedom that it spins itself to the turning of the wheel."

A cold chill crawled across Aurelie's flesh.

Sera narrowed her eyes. "There are so many objects in this room that we could use as the mother-of-all. But perhaps the simplest way will just be for one of us to hold the spindle while the other turns the wheel. Do you have a preference?"

"Stop this!" Aurelie said. "Stop this now! Stop pretending that you are against me. I don't need a lesson right now. I need you. My friend. My Sera." She held out her arms, willing Sera to fling away the corrupted objects and run to her.

Sera took a step toward her. "I told you," she said. "My name is not Sera."

Aurelie let out a small, moaning cry.

Sera's perpetual face-scrunching smile had dropped away, and her face smoothed like a cracked and aged slab of granite. She pulled off her wimple, and a thick torrent of graying-brown hair cascaded down her back. For the first time, she stood straight and tall without a hunch, and the light of the afternoon sun shone through the stained-glass window like a halo around her head. She looked haggard and unearthly and powerful. "It's time for one last revelation," she said, her voice sounding smooth and stentorian. "I am Seraphine of the Jura, spinner of magic and mother of the king's first child. My life is bound to a vow that I must keep today before sunset."

Grief and rage surged through Aurelie. "No," she said. "You cannot be her. You are Sera, mon amie. You are practically my mother."

"But I am not you mother," Seraphine said. "It is a difference of blood. Blood matters."

Aurelie wept.

"So, I do get tears now, after all?" Seraphine said, with a soft smile. "Do not worry, Princess. I might not be your mother, but I am the guardian of your destiny, and I have brought you to this moment with care, and I have prepared you to play your part."

Aurelie glared. She wanted to rub the tears off her face, but she could not reach. "So," she said, "all my life—all our relationship—has been a lie?"

"I did not lie!" Seraphine snapped, her calm breaking like a river bursting through the ice of winter. "I am the only person who has ever told you the truth. Even in the fairy tales I have always pointed you toward the greater truth."

"But I loved you!" Aurelie cried.

Seraphine's jaw flexed. "Some debts are stronger than love."

"I don't believe that," Aurelie said. "I know you love me too. You have always taken care of me, listened to me. You are the one who made sure I grew up with books and games. You taught me the lore and the ways of our country." Aurelie cast about the room, trying to find more proofs, but her eyes widened suddenly, and her breath caught in her throat. "And yet, you have always been there irritating my parents, bit by bit, driving a wedge between them and me. You were the one who pushed my father away today. And you kept my mother in the room so you could take away her pin. Then you tricked me into staying with you when I was ready to leave." Aurelie took a step back. "You are a monster!"

Seraphine flinched. "Don't overthink this," she said. "I am an agent of justice."

"I don't believe that," Aurelie said. "I don't believe anything you say." She moved back toward the door and pressed her ear against it. She wondered if anyone was close enough to hear her if she called.

"Don't you understand yet, Princess?" Seraphine said.

Aurelie looked at her and pondered how much force it would take to overpower the determined old woman and wrestle back the key.

"Exploitation and greed!" Seraphine said.

How much speed and agility would it take to unlock the door, Aurelie considered, and then run down the stairs in a royal gown?

"Adultery and Betrayal!" Seraphine said.

Most importantly, Aurelie thought, how many times could Seraphine strike her with the pin before she managed to get away?

"Torture and murder!" Seraphine said. "Your parents have compromised in every way. Now they need to pay, and the price has been set. They had sixteen years to make amends for their ways, to try to redeem you. But all they did was lock you in a tower and look the other way. That's why the kingdom is cursed. That's why my vow has to be fulfilled today. To teach everyone a lesson." Seraphine's hands clenched. "Do you want to help me, Princess? Or do you want to watch the Free Country fall?"

Aurelie shook her head, breathing in quick, shallow gasps. "You are no better than they," she said. "Betrayal for betrayal.

There is no way you can possibly justify what you are doing to me."

"You are only alive because I summoned you," Seraphine said. "You are the product of their compromise, the child of black magic, cursed before your christening. I have a claim—a right—to your blood." Hunger sparked in her eyes. "But that does not really matter because I do not need to betray you." She smirked. "By the end of the day, Princess, you will make this choice for yourself. You will offer your own blood on my spindle."

Aurelie let out a sharp laugh. The lie was so ludicrous—that she, the princess locked in the tower, was the one who actually had the power to choose whether to live or die this day. And then she seized on the idea and held it to her heart, like an ember kindling a flame. If she had a choice, then she was going to live. Today, she—if no one else—would ensure her own survival.

"You are a good princess," Seraphine said, "and that's why I know that you will help me in the end." Aurelie could tell that Seraphine believed what she said. "You will rise above the low conditions of your birth. You will choose to do what is right." The older woman reached out her powerful, gnarly hands, beckoning.

Aurelie's heart pounded. "I intend to be something more than a good princess," she said. She took a step forward, and she felt the heavy swish of her dress, and she knew then that it was designed for only one purpose—to stand in power. "I will be a good queen," she said.

Seraphine's eyes narrowed.

"I am only just beginning to see the complexity of my task," Aurelie said, "my role in leading the Free Country. But I am also beginning to understand what you said about power." She held out her hands, reaching for her adversary, her friend, and she caught the knobby palms and felt a pulse of energy pass between them. "I am not afraid of the weight of your ideas, Seraphine." She squeezed the old, familiar hands. "My first work as leader will be to make atonement for your lost child."

Seraphine flinched.

"I know that I cannot replace a human life," Aurelie said. "But I can acknowledge the loss. And then I can review the laws and systems that allowed such a tragedy to happen. I can change those things. I can't make a perfect kingdom, but I can make one that values human life above gain. I will not accept that some people should be exploited or abused so that others can live. There will never be a quota of human suffering that has to be filled. We will find room and wealth and healing enough for everyone." Aurelie's voice sounded sonorous and strong, and her eyes glistened with conviction. "From the moment I leave this tower, I will begin working toward this kind of a good and just foundation in the Free Country, and I will keep working until I have built it stone by stone. Will you help me?"

Seraphine trembled. She pulled her hands away from Aurelie's and crossed her arms. "You're still so naïve," she sneered. "Do you think your parents would share their lives or their power with a witch?"

Aurelie winced. "I only know this," she said. "Your life and mine can have a greater purpose than ending together inside this tower. You've said it yourself so many times—there is always another way."

Seraphine frowned, her hairless brows furrowing.

"I am ready to forgive you," Aurelie said, holding out her hand. "Can you accept that?"

Seraphine stared at the hand. "Like you promised to forgive the bad choices of your father?" she said. "Like you promised to ignore and justify whatever he did?"

Aurelie flushed, and she lost herself for a moment in that memory as it took on a new meaning. Had her father really been talking about killing his own child? Aurelie shook her head, trying to focus on her own goals and beliefs—her own life that needed to be saved right now. "There is a path forward for all of us," she said. "I believe that forgiveness is part of that."

Seraphine looked away. "Your words are pretty," she said, her voice dry and emotionless. "But they have no power behind them. Mine are made of blood and mountain. A bargain was struck, a deal made, and I cannot change my part in it now. Even if I tried, you would not escape. None of your family would. No one in the kingdom would escape." She gritted her teeth. "Because one way or another, the Devil will come to collect. And he doesn't mind if he drowns only one rat or the whole nest."

Aurelie shuddered, feeling weakened by a wave of horror. She opened her mouth to say something, anything, to counter this idea—to deny this curse.

Seraphine held up her hand. "Evil is more powerful than good, Princess. You have to know when to serve it if you want to survive." She patted the bone pin still stuck across her heart. "All you need to do is prick your finger."

Aurelie's sweat turned cold, as though an icy breath had blown across her. She tried to think of new arguments, but nothing came to mind. All she could think about was that old, lifelong dread that the Devil was coming for her and that he really did have a claim on her soul. She moved backward, conscious of nothing but the desire to put space between herself and Seraphine, and her feet stumbled over something hard, the fallen chessboard.

Aurelie snatched it up, holding it out like a shield. "Listen to me, Seraphine," she said. "I intend to live, and if you want, you can still make it out of this tower alive too. Do you really think that trading my soul to the Devil will spare your own?"

Seraphine grinned so that her teeth showed. "Maybe it will," she said. "Maybe he will preserve my life along with yours, and I will remain here with you, feeding you bits of bread and water as you sleep for all eternity."

"No!" Aurelie cried. She wanted to hurl the chessboard at Seraphine's grinning face. "Don't you understand?" Aurelie said. "I am trying to save you as much as I am trying to save myself."

"Save me from what?" Seraphine said. "From your little chessboard?"

"From being thrown off the parapet!" Aurelie said. "From being rolled down the hill in a barrel full of nails. If you persist, I will call for help, and they will come running, and no one will show you any mercy." Aurelie let out an angry groan. "Don't you understand? You have the key. You can leave now and go wherever you want and never come back." Hot tears welled in her eyes, and she blinked them back. "I'll tell them a story about you. People will think you are a hero." Aurelie started to weep, and she gritted her teeth. "Choose life. Choose it for both of us."

A soft smile passed over Seraphine's face. "I like that," she said. "I like that you tried to save me. In all the times I played this day out in my mind, I never imagined that." She looked at the pieces of her half-constructed spinning wheel. "I could just walk away now, couldn't I? The kingdom might fall. You might go with it, impaled on a sword instead of a spindle. But I could walk away free." She looked up at Aurelie, and her eyes glinted, cold and hard as two stones. "Only I would rather die than let your parents go unpunished for what they've done."

Aurelie's eyes widened, staring. Then she turned and smashed the chessboard against the door, breaking the wooden board in half. The door remained firm. Aurelie ran to it and pounded against the heavy slab. "Father! Mother! Sir Roland!" The words ripped from her throat, and her voice, unused to shouting, broke and sounded unnatural and flimsy. "Help me!" she shouted. "Someone! Help me!" She swiveled and slammed her back against the door. It did not even shift. She panted, struggling to regain her breath, and she kept her eyes on Seraphine as she listened for the sound of running feet.

No one answered. No one came.

Aurelie gathered the fabric of her red skirt.

Seraphine watched her with half-closed eyes. "I have waited all day for someone to rescue you," she said softly. "I almost hoped they would."

Aurelie uttered a strangled cry and leapt forward. Seraphine stumbled back, hugging the wheel to her chest. Aurelie collided with her and seized the wheel, trying to wrench it free. She shoved, rocking Seraphine back, trying to break her grip.

"Let go now," Aurelie said. "Or I'll break the window, and all the kingdom will come running."

Seraphine teetered, still clinging to the wheel. But she had the advantage of wearing light clothing made for labor. She dug one foot into the ground and kicked Aurelie hard in the gut.

Aurelie gasped and staggered back, catching her foot on the red dress. She fell, hitting the floor. Her vision exploded in sparks, and her breath left her body. She seized up, trying to get air. Then she rolled onto her face and pushed up on her knees, gasping and shuddering. Her hair had come out of its intricate weave, a wreckage of loops and braids falling across her face and shoulders. One of her sleeves had torn, and she yanked it off. With one arm free, she ripped at the old laces binding her dress, and she snapped the knots, taking a deep gasp of warm, stifling air.

"I always loved this window," Seraphine said. She gazed at the stained glass as if capturing a memory of beauty. Then she raised the food platter high over her head and dashed it against the window. The clear central pane shattered outward in a burst of shards. Cracks split through the painted panes, splintering out from the center, severing saints to the music of a thousand tiny tinkles and pings. Then the rainbow-colored glass began to fall in a shower of knife-sharp fragments, shattering on the windowsill and strewing across the stone floor.

Aurelie threw up her arms, huddling to protect herself. Wind rushed in through the open window, carrying the sharp smells of earth, dung, smoke, spices and mountains. She gasped, drinking in deep breaths of cool, fresh air, like a baby, like a starving woman, laughing and crying at the sharp and liberating taste. A roar of sound filled her ears, but she could not make out what it was. She looked up and rose slowly to her feet. The beautiful glass window was gone. Across the gap, the frames of leaden lattice remained, like the web of a giant spider.

Seraphine looked back over her shoulder. Blood oozed from gashes along the older woman's cheek and forearm. She smiled. "Go ahead," she said. "Call for help."

Aurelie blinked in confusion. Then she ran forward, stepping around the glass. "Help!" she shouted. Her voice still sounded too small, but it was warming up. "Help me!" She pushed past Seraphine and leaned out across the hazardous sill to gaze down at the sea of movement in the courtyard below. People swarmed like ants. Horses whinnied. Trumpets blasted. Nobles shouted and argued about the placement of their things and people. Knights of competing loyalties clashed shields with each other and flirted with women of various ranks. Children chased dogs and chickens and ran away from the geese and parents. Horses were led one way and another, getting jammed where the crowd was too packed and dropping shit where they stood. Actors juggled and played music. Jesters cracked wise. And underneath it all there was a familiar, terrible sense of urgency. Aurelie noticed the guards and king's men rushing around and corralling people into groups. Battalions of soldiers poured out of the open front gate and ran through the city and lined the bridges.

Why all the soldiers? Aurelie wondered. *Why the maneuvering?* Heart sinking, she lifted her gaze to that far off group she'd glimpsed before, journeying toward her city. It was crossing the valley now, cast in the shadow of the hills and trampling the fields, now empty of peasants. Rank and file of armored riders and soldiers approached. And over the whole massive group fluttered the blue and yellow banners of the Duchy.

Aurelie gazed at the sun, still so far from setting, and she felt as though some enemy catapult had smashed a hole through her heart. For the first time, she wondered if what Seraphine had said might be true—if sacrificing herself was somehow the only hope for survival. Because this day really did carry a curse for her whole kingdom. It brought war. And she, Aurelie, might be the last player standing between the Free Country and the Devil's final move.

Seraphine whistled, and Aurelie returned sharply to the present. She gathered her skirts and stepped up onto the windowsill and reached for the leaden web. It bent and crumbled under her grasp. She cried out and steadied herself against the wall. "Help me!" she shouted. "The sorceress is here! She's trying to kill me!" Her voice got lost in the noise of the crowd.

Directly below the tower, a noblewoman looked up. She had a wimple twisted like horns over each ear and lips painted blood red. She gazed up at Aurelie for a moment, and then she shook her fist and pointed at a pile of trunks that had been showered in glass. She began shouting instructions to some servants, who jumped up and used their hats and coats to wipe the trunks clean.

"Help me!" Aurelie pleaded, falling to her knees on the sill. But the woman ignored her. The servants did not seem to hear—or they chose not to listen. Seraphine had gotten up on the sill beside her, and Aurelie dimly became aware of the words she was shouting above the cacophony. "You foolish wench! The king will have someone's head when he sees this mess you've made of the window. Yes, go on, cry for help. The king's men will beat you more fiercely than I will when they discover this. Go on. Stop complaining and clean it up."

Aurelie looked up at her old friend, her guardian, and the pieces of her mind felt like they were coming apart, breaking like the glass of the window, unable to survive a world out-side the tower—or in it.

"You see it now, don't you?" Seraphine said, looking down. "The curse is coming to a head here in this place today. The gods are thirsty for blood. And so, war is upon the Free Country. And the nobles are only feeding their bellies and their egos on the brink of destruction. If you do not do your part now and show us all what it means to be good, to value justice above self-gain and virtue above your own freedom, then this doom will devour us all."

Aurelie groaned. Her vision blurred. She strained to focus, staring at the few jagged edges of glass still jutting from the lattice, and there, in front of her, was the head of the dragon. Marguerite's dress dripped from its mouth like a wide, silky tongue. An ache formed in Aurelie's stomach, as though she had eaten a bad fruit. She wanted to do right, but she no longer knew what that was.

Seraphine opened her mouth, that display of broken and missing teeth, and she laughed. The sound was melodic and cold, nothing like the wheezing cackles she used to make. Aurelie shuddered and looked up, understanding that she was glimpsing the real Seraphine for perhaps the first time. Seraphine wiped her dry eyes, chuckling mirthlessly, and she slid down to sit next to Aurelie. "Words," she said, as if she were still the mentor and Aurelie her pupil. "Words matter so very much. They can move mountains. They can topple kingdoms. And they can cause a whole crowd of people to look the other way when something horrendous is happening. I've seen it so many times before. If only I had understood the power of words sooner. I could have gone so much farther than this." She gestured to the room.

Aurelie stared, reeling at this new vision of her old friend, relaxed, authoritative and pitiless.

"Oh, I do understand the irony," Seraphine said. "Trapping myself in this tower. Deforming my body beyond what they already did to me so that it hurts now to stand up straight. Hiding my voice, my ideas, from all but a little girl." She sighed. "I was so arrogant and angry that day when I cursed you—still so young, too, in my own way. I might have just cursed you to die then and walked away free. But I wanted everyone to remember my words. I wanted my words to haunt and cripple them and change them forever. I wanted her to feel it most of all. And she did. She has. She withered—inside and out." Seraphine laughed. "She used to love her spinning and her weaving more than anything. That's why I took it away from her—along with the love of her only daughter."

Aurelie trembled at the cruelty of the words. But a strong, fresh breeze blew against her cheek, and she took in deep breaths, receiving strength. The sun warmed her face, and in the plain light, she could see her old friend clearly: the broken nose, the lips caving in where teeth were missing, the blotched and sun-deprived skin, smeared with charcoal and lined with gruesome scars. But Aurelie also saw the high arch of her plucked brow, the curve of her lip and the gleam of her hazel eyes. The large hands softly stroked the wheel.

"You are enjoying this," Aurelie said.

"What?"

"You're not an agent of justice," Aurelie said. "You only want revenge."

Seraphine's nostrils flared. "You don't know what you're talking about."

"I wonder if you even believe your curse has any power," Aurelie said. "That's why you're fighting so hard to make it happen. What you really want is to break me the way you were once broken. You want me to destroy myself just as you have been destroying yourself all this time. And you think that will mean that you have won."

"How dare you!" Seraphine said. "You are a girl in a tower. You know nothing." Her lips quivered for a moment, and then she choked out a harsh laugh. "So, maybe I do want revenge. So what? It doesn't change what I said about the curse. It's still going to destroy you one way or another." She leaned forward. "And let me tell you something about yourself, Princess. No matter how this day ends, you have already lost. Because you are not a good princess. I knew it when I woke up last night to an empty tower. I knew it when you cried no tears for me today. Your heart has already begun to compromise—to rot. You are nothing like the lotus. You cannot come out of this clean."

Aurelie winced, wounded though she knew that she should not care about what this woman said of her.

Seraphine stood up. "Even your parents knew they needed to let you go and start over," she said. She walked to the bed, her bare foot tracking blood through the glass. She tossed away the yellow blanket and peeled back the fur, and then she picked up a shard of glass and slashed through the cloth-lined mattress. A bulge of white wool spilled out, and Aurelie smelled the pungent odor of animal grease. Seraphine pulled out a gob. "Here is one last truth, Princess," she said, holding it up. "They themselves have given me all the tools I need to do this."

Aurelie trembled. The new information and sounds and smells combined like an assault, threatening to overwhelm her senses. She felt faint, and she looked down and saw the food, tossed from the platter, squished on the ground, and nausea added to her pain. She told herself that she should try to eat some of it and get back her strength, but she knew that no matter what she put in her mouth, she would not be able to swallow. She turned back to the window to catch that wind on her face again, but when she reached out to balance herself, more of the lattice crumbled away, and she gasped, clutching at air.

Far below, a jester made a crowd burst into raucous laughter. A servant scolded another servant, tossing off his hat. A goose screamed as someone plucked its tail feather. And there, approaching the bridges that crossed the river that wrapped around the city like a shield, the army from the Duchy marched on.

Aurelie closed her eyes, trying to focus, trying to find hope and a way out. Then her ears caught a tiny sound. It was the one sound she had trained her whole life to hear. It was the sound of the lower tower door scraping open.

A footstep landed on the first stair.

8

Pater Noster

A hard, wooden object clunked onto the stair, and Aurelie knew that she had been given a way out—a chance to save both her body and soul. She gathered up her skirt and stepped down from the windowsill and through the mosaic of food and shattered glass. "Seraphine," she said, "I am ready to help you now."

Seraphine was humming a whining tune and combing her fingers through the matted wool that she'd pulled out of the mattress. She looked up, confused. "That's it? No more struggle? You just suddenly want to help me now?"

"Yes," Aurelie said. "I understand what's at stake." She spoke loudly, trying to cover the thump and shuffle of the person on the stair. "What are you doing there? Why did you cut open the mattress?"

"I need wool to spin thread," Seraphine said. "A spinning wheel spins wool into thread. This is really not that hard to understand, Princess. I wonder why you—" Seraphine froze, listening. Then she leapt to her feet. A heartbeat later, she had pressed a shard of glass to Aurelie's throat.

Aurelie held still, not breathing.

In the quiet, a staff thudded on the stair, and two footsteps shuffled after.

"I know that step," Seraphine said, wrapping her arm around Aurelie's waist.

"I know it too," Aurelie said. "And it means that you have failed. You will be exposed. God has stopped you."

"I wouldn't be so sure," Seraphine said, and a smile played on her lips. "Let us call a truce for now, you and I. We will let the blind bishop come inside but tell him nothing. If you want, you may make a last confession. And then, when he leaves, we will finish this."

The hobbling step drew closer.

"Why would I do that?" Aurelie hissed.

"Because otherwise," Seraphine said, "I will kill you. Or him." She brushed her cheek against Aurelie's. "I'm very keen to deliver this—as you call it—revenge. You can choose how."

Aurelie suppressed a shudder. "Very well," she said. "For now."

The step reached the top of the stair, and the visitor knocked.

Seraphine nodded, loosening her grip and stepping back.

"Is that you, Father Aimery?" Aurelie called. Her throat felt so dry.

"It is I," the bishop said, his voice a cheerful wheeze. He fumbled his key into the lock and turned it.

Seraphine held out Aurelie's half-key, and Aurelie jammed it into her side of the lock and flung open the door. "Bonjour Father Aimery!"

"My goodness!" Father Aimery said, leaning on his long, pastoral staff and clutching at the doorframe. His cloudy blue eyes roved across the ceiling, and his reddish-skinned neck jutted forward like a russet hen's. The bishop's mitre on top of his head wobbled, and he caught it and wedged it under one arm. "Bonjour mesdames," he said, chuckling and rubbing at the ring of soft gray hairs around his bare head. "Is now a good time for a visit? I could come back—"

"No, please, come in," Aurelie said, taking his hand and pulling him inside. "I am very glad to see you." Behind the bishop, the empty staircase yawned open.

"That's a relief," Father Aimery said. "This tower stair is a long trek. I would hate to tell my knees they had walked it for nothing."

"Of course," Aurelie said, glancing back at the open door. "Thank you." She kicked a silver coin out of the bishop's way.

"What was that?" Father Aimery said, tilting his head.

"Nothing," Aurelie said.

Seraphine shut the door and relieved him of his staff.

Father Aimery's unseeing eyes rolled toward the window. "My child, is everything all right? I heard a terrible crash on my way here, and there is a knight down there who said he heard it too, only he is too polite to visit a lady's chamber on his own. He asked me to check on you first." Father Aimery chuckled. "What manners!"

Aurelie's face flushed, but she kept her voice calm. "Everything is fine, Father," she said. "Nothing crashed."

"That's good," Father Aimery said. "But, pardon my asking, why do I feel a draft?"

"It's the—the fireplace," Aurelie stammered.

"She is afraid to tell you the truth, your Excellency," Seraphine cut in. Her old smiles and creaky voice had returned. "Our lovely window was broken. We were cleaning the room one last time, and we pushed too hard on the glass."

"My goodness!" Father Aimery said. "What a loss. I understand that window was a great testament to Christian sacrifice. But, Madame Sera was right to tell me the truth, dear child. You should always take refuge in the truth." He squeezed Aurelie's arm, then turned back, feeling for the door. "So, if there is really nothing amiss, then I will just tell Sir Roland. I don't want to keep him waiting."

"He is at the bottom of the stair, your Excellency?" Seraphine said.

"Yes, yes," Bishop Aimery said. "At the bottom of the stair."

Seraphine opened the door and offered her own arm for the bishop to lean on. She still held his staff, and blood dripped from the cut in her forearm and pooled where her fingers gripped the handle.

"Everything is all right, Sir Roland!" Father Aimery called. "You may return to your post."

"Thank you, your Excellency!" Roland called up. "But I wish to come up and speak with the princess myself, if I may."

"Oh?" Father Aimery said.

"I—I must apologize to her," Roland said.

"Oh?" Father Aimery said again, turning back to the women and raising his eyebrows.

Aurelie's heart pounded. Her senses whirled. "Yes!" she shouted. "Please, come up now, Sir Roland! Make haste!" She seized the bishop's arm and pulled him hard, toward herself, away from Seraphine.

Bishop Aimery let out a squawk and jerked away, catching at the door. "My goodness, the youth!" he said.

Seraphine clamped a hand down on his shoulder. "There, there," she said. She helped him tuck his mitre back under his arm. "I've got you." Then she turned toward Aurelie with a look that that could have cracked stones.

Aurelie quailed.

"Thank you, your highness!" Sir Roland shouted. His footsteps leapt up the first few steps, then slowed, as if he were trying to pace himself. "Don't worry," he called up. "I have left behind my sword."

Seraphine smiled. "Is meeting this young man today really worth so much to you?" she said. She drew a shard of glass from her pocket and held it a finger's length away from the bishop's jutting throat.

"No," Aurelie whispered. She wished Sir Roland had moved faster. She wished she had screamed. She wished that Father Aimery had trusted her enough to move with her and so given her at least a fighting chance to save them both. Now she could only save one. "Stop!" Aurelie shouted. "Do not come a step closer, Sir Roland. I have changed my mind." Her voice choked on the words, and she realized that she probably sounded to Roland like a petulant young coquette, unsure of what she wanted. A crazed, anguished laugh bubbled up from deep inside, and she doubled over, covering her mouth to stifle it.

Roland's footsteps stopped.

Aurelie rocked with silent laughter, though her heart felt crushed beyond any sense of humor, beyond any thought but the will to survive—and to not kill anyone else in the process.

"As you wish, lady," Roland said. "Only please let me apologize to you from here."

Aurelie couldn't speak. She closed her eyes and pressed her palms against her face to stop the laughter, to stop the tears.

"I behaved like a fool earlier," Roland said. His voice was so close. He had only to run up ten more steps, and he could have saved her. He had only to break the rules of his manners, his chivalry. "Perhaps I was wrong to visit you, to offer you my service in the first place," Roland said. "I do not know. But it was worse for me to go back on my word and leave you here alone and distressed and possibly even ashamed by my abandonment. Nothing can excuse such a callous lack of chivalry. Will you forgive me?"

Aurelie sighed. She had regained her calm in the midst of Roland's impassioned speech. "I forgive you," she said quietly. She felt sorry for this knight who was so afraid to do good. But she also despised him. He had fought so very hard to win her forgiveness. "Now, please, go," she said. And because she felt a little pity for him, she added: "My feelings and my fate are no longer your concern. I have already released you from your pledge of service."

"I do not ask to be released again, lady," Roland said. "I would still serve you today."

Aurelie sighed and closed her eyes. "Then go fetch me a pitcher of water and leave it at the bottom of the stair for when I go out," she said. "I am so thirsty."

Roland was quiet for a moment. "Might I just come up and speak with you?"

"No," Aurelie said. She guided Father Aimery away from the door and pushed it closed, its hinges groaning.

"I smelled only fire!" Roland shouted.

"What?" Aurelie paused, holding the door open a crack.

"The queen mentioned a stench," Roland said. "It must have embarrassed you. But I wanted you to know that I noticed only the smell of burning peat. And then roses."

Aurelie smiled. Then she closed the door. She leaned her head against it and listened to Roland's footsteps descending. The lower tower door scraped shut.

Father Aimery coughed. "My child," he said, reaching for Aurelie, and she moved so that he did not touch her arm where the sleeve had been torn off. "I am glad that you are guarding your heart," Father Aimery said. "But you will find few men with such excellent manners as Sir Roland!"

Aurelie took the bishop's stiff, dry hand and squeezed it. She could not speak.

"So," Father Aimery said, patting her hand. "Today you leave the tower. Do you feel quite happy?"

"Yes, Father," Aurelie said, fighting back the urge to cry.

"Very good," Father Aimery said. "Would you like some company to pass the time? I have gotten my hands on a book by Hildegard von Bingen. She was a German abbess who lived much of her life in isolation, like you. She wrote music and books of science. She even penned letters to the Pope!" Father Aimery pulled a small volume out of his robes. "Have I piqued your interest?"

Aurelie studied him. "You would choose to stay with me here today, Father Aimery?"

"Why not?" Father Aimery said, smiling. "You are one of my favorite readers."

"You are not afraid of the curse?" Aurelie said. She could feel the malice of Seraphine, standing too close to her shoulder.

"I do not fear pagan nonsense," Father Aimery said.

A knot tightened in Aurelie's stomach, and she no longer felt the urge to cry.

"Here," Father Aimery said, pressing the book into her hands. "Tell me what it looks like."

Aurelie turned back the leather cover. "It's penned with black ink," she said. "The first letter of this page has swirls, like vines. And there is a sketch of a plant. The handwriting is small, and the words sort of run into the margins."

"She must have had so much to say!" Father Aimery said, rubbing his hands together.

Seraphine cleared her throat.

Aurelie handed back the book. "Today I will just make a confession," she said, "and then I would like to be left alone."

"Of course," Father Aimery said, but he pushed the book back into her hand. "Why don't you keep it for now?" Aurelie supported him as he knelt and placed his mitre back on his head. Then Aurelie knelt beside him. In front of them, on the ground, lay the queen's wimple, dirty and spotted with blood.

Seraphine grunted and finally moved away to sit at the windowsill. There she leaned the bishop's staff against her shoulder like a spinner's distaff. Wind blew long strands of her graying-brown hair across her face as she took her combed wool and began twisting the straightened fibers into a loose cord between her bloodied hands.

Aurelie's imagination flew. She could make her escape right now while Seraphine was occupied and the door was unlocked. She, Aurelie, could leap up and dash through, and then she could run down the stairs and throw open the bottom door and call for help. Surely Roland or someone would hear her and help her when they saw Seraphine following, dripping with blood. Yet then Aurelie would have to leave the blind bishop alone and defenseless in the tower. And she could not do that. Her heart beat painfully fast.

"Your Excellency," Seraphine said, startling them both. She was rubbing the cord of wool between her bloodstained hands and wrapping it around the curving top of the staff.

"Yes, Madame Sera?" Father Aimery said.

"Your Excellency, would you sacrifice your life for someone else?" Seraphine said.

Father Aimery coughed and scratched his ear. "Pardon me?"

"Isn't that the most noble deed of all?" Seraphine said. "Dying for some other person or cause? And wouldn't you almost be obligated to do it if your sacrifice could save a lot of people—or even just one person as precious as our sweet Aurelie here?" Her voice squeaked in the old, kindly way, but she was grinning like a wolf.

Aurelie stared down at the queen's wimple, the silver coins scattered all around it.

Father Aimery shifted and rubbed his knees. "Hmm. You ladies always have such inquiring minds!" He cleared his throat. "The answer, for me, is of course, yes," he said. "As a bishop, my job is to lay down my life every day for my precious children of the faith. But most of the time I accomplish that on my sorry old knees." He chuckled and held up a finger. "Non adversus carnem."

"You must forgive an old servant woman," Seraphine said. "Carnem?" She wrapped another length of the cord around the bishop's staff.

"Ah, yes," Father Aimery said. "Carnem—flesh. Of course, we must be careful not to sully the holy words by translating them into the vulgar tongue. However, I think I can still express the idea to a curious and devoted mind. You see, our battle is not fought in a physical realm but in a spiritual one. That is where I die every day."

"Do the crusaders know that?" Seraphine said, cocking her head. "Maybe someone should tell them."

"Ah ha!" Father Aimery said. "You have such a keen mind, madame. The crusaders are dying in the flesh for their faith, just as our blessed Christ did. There is no greater testament to Christendom."

"What about the heretics, Jews and Saracens, then?" Seraphine said. "What are their deaths a testament to?"

"My goodness!" Father Aimery said, starting to get up, then stopping himself. "You must be careful, madame. You must not allow the agility of your wit to carry you into the realms of heresy." He rubbed his knees. "Now, we are here for confession! What would you like to confess, my child?"

Aurelie stared at the dripping trail of blood streaking across the queen's wimple, and she wished she had more time. Just time. She wanted to ponder all the things she had ever heard and separate who had said each and with what motivation so that she could figure out now what she really believed was true. But there was no time. Beyond the threat of Seraphine waving around shards of glass, there was also an army of soldiers marching on the Free Country, moving toward her beloved city. Aurelie reeled, wondering if she might really have the power, bedded within the curse, to protect her whole kingdom from that doom. She felt so alone and afraid and tired, but she could not share a word of it with the bishop if she wanted him to walk out of the room alive. She wondered what it would feel like to die today—or to sleep and never wake. She mourned the fact that she had never truly left the tower. She had grown up in captivity for seemingly no purpose at all. She had never even smelled a real rose.

And then she felt glad, suddenly, that she had reached out and touched Sir Roland's hand—even if he had let go and gone away.

"I suppose you will want to confess your lie?" Father Aimery said.

"What?" Aurelie said, looking up, startled.

The bishop's blue eyes gazed straight into her own. "The truth that you attempted to conceal," he said.

Aurelie tried to calm her rapid breathing. Had the bishop figured out what was happening? Would she be able to stop Seraphine from killing him? "I don't know—"

"Breaking the window?" Father Aimery prompted. "Lying about it?"

"Oh, yes!" Aurelie said. Relief surged through her already overwhelmed senses. "The window, yes, the window. I lied about it. Yes, I did. But that's not all! That's not all I want to confess. There are many, many sins I want to confess." In fact, she wanted to confess every last sin and half-sin that she might have ever committed so that in case she could not save her body today she would at least save her soul. But, for the life of her, Aurelie could not think of a single sin. She pinched herself, trying to clear her head by channeling her feelings of inner torment into the twisting skin of her forearm.

Seraphine stopped wrapping wool around her staff and stared, her mouth forming a hard line across her face. Father Aimery scratched his head and cleared his throat. "Yes?" he said. A fly entered the room and buzzed. A bit of peat popped on the fire. Aurelie wanted to live if it killed her. "Father!" she cried, finding the words at last. "I doubt."

"You doubt?" Father Aimery said, jumping a little.

Seraphine shifted forward, watching them.

"Yes, Father, I doubt," Aurelie said. "I doubt everything. I doubt that the things I grew up believing are true. I doubt that my parents love me. I doubt the clear nature of good versus evil. Maybe I even doubt you, too, in a way, just because I doubt everything else. And, of course, I doubt myself most of all. I doubt that I am good, or that I know what is good. And I doubt God. I doubt that God actually has any kind of real power or control. Otherwise, I must doubt that God is good."

Aurelie took a deep breath and sagged.

Seraphine smiled.

Father Aimery frowned, but he reached for Aurelie's hand and squeezed it, a little too tightly. "For one so young to struggle with so much—"

Hope blazed in Aurelie's heart—the hope that she was not alone, the hope that she would find the answers she needed today, the hope that she could still escape. "Can you help me, Father?" she said, voice trembling.

Father Aimery cleared his throat. "You have done right to bring this to me and to God. It is not a great sin to struggle with doubt if you share your struggle with God himself." He fell silent.

Aurelie waited, hanging on his words.

"And so," Father Aimery said, "I shall assign you only a light penance. We will say the pater noster, and you will be absolved."

"That's it?" Aurelie asked.

"Yes, one pater noster is enough."

"No, I mean, can you not tell me—"

Father Aimery raised his eyebrows. Seraphine shook her head.

"Never mind, Father," Aurelie said.

"Let us begin the prayer together, shall we?" Father Aimery said. "We must remember—as we pray to our father in heaven and ask for his will to come to pass—that we can release all our doubts and trust him with whatever happens next. Amen?"

"Amen, Father," Aurelie said. She glanced at Seraphine, who was smiling again.

The bishop stretched out his neck, straightening his mitre, and he began to pray.

"Pater noster

qui es in caelis

sanctificetur nomen tuum."

As he prayed, Aurelie followed along, quietly, earnestly, willing the words, like a good spell, to come true.

"Adveniat regnum tuum

fiat voluntas tua

sicut in caelo et in terra."

"There," Father Aimery said when they had finished the prayer. "Don't you feel better?"

Aurelie couldn't speak. Tears splashed down her cheeks, and she did not want to give them away by sobbing. Finally, she found breath and words. "But Father," she said, "I still doubt."

"Oh." Father Aimery frowned and cocked his head. He reached out for a moment, and his hand gently brushed across her wet cheek. "I see," he said. He seemed to glance about the room, and his breath wheezed, shallow and agitated.

Seraphine tensed. She gripped the wool-wrapped staff and picked up a shard of glass.

Father Aimery's head lowered toward his chest. "You must ask yourself a question, Princess," he said. "What do you want? What do you want more than anything else in the whole world?"

Aurelie steadied, moved deeply by the question that no one had ever asked her before. She wiped the tears from her face. She wanted to live. That much she knew. And she wanted to lead her country well. But, she realized now, between those two obvious goals, there must be a chasm filled with far more personal, more intimate wishes that spoke of her very deepest self. How could she open her heart enough to answer such a question now? Yet she must. She must because she knew instinctively that if she could find the answer to this question, then she could also find a way to make it out of the tower alive today. A vision brightened in her mind—peasants dancing around bonfires in the hills. But how could she put that into words?

"The question," Father Aimery said, raising his head, "is do you want to live for yourself, satisfying your own selfish desires, or do you want to please God?"

Aurelie stiffened.

"Because if you want to do good," the bishop continued, "then you will have to sacrifice your own desires. You must honor your parents. You must work hard for the kingdom. You must serve the church. One day you will have to submit to your husband, who will be king. You will have to learn every day to suppress your own feelings and desires in order to serve your country and support all those around you who deserve your loyalty. As a princess, you must choose to live above reproach."

Aurelie listened, immobilized, and when Father Aimery started to rise, she did not stir, so he dug his hand into her shoulder and pushed himself up. "We will address the question of doubt again at your next confession," he said.

"Don't worry. You do not have to carry this burden alone." He turned and felt for the door.

Seraphine was there in a moment, holding a shard of glass close to his unprotected neck. Aurelie shook herself and rose and opened the door.

Father Aimery turned toward Aurelie suddenly, almost cutting his own throat. "I almost forgot," he said, reaching for her hand and gripping it. "I came here to warn you of a danger that you will face very soon."

"Please, don't," Aurelie said, pushing him out the door and onto the landing. "Please, tell me later." She did not feel that she could keep up her lie much longer. She did not want to see Bishop Aimery cut down on her threshold.

Father Aimery tightened his grip on her hand. "Wait," he said. "I must tell you now."

"No, I'm sure that you can tell me later," Aurelie said, making herself a wall between Seraphine and the bishop. Seraphine's shard of glass moved from the bishop's throat to Aurelie's.

"I must speak with you specifically about how you leave the tower today and prepare for a new life outside," Father Aimery said.

Aurelie did not answer. Her legs trembled.

"Do tell us," Seraphine said.

Aurelie shuddered. She felt weak and tired, but she maintained the wall, and she waited for the bishop to talk himself into their doom.

"I am sorry to be the one to tell you this," Father Aimery said. "But you must know so you can guard yourself. As soon as you leave this tower, Princess Aurelie, you are going to face the awful peril of fashion."

"What?" Aurelie said, a knee buckling in her shock.

"Yes," Father Aimery said. "Fashion. It is one of the Devil's trickiest traps, his gateway sin into Hell. You see, young men and young women unwittingly follow the impulses of lust, greed and competition to dress themselves in more and more frivolous and provocative clothing. They think it is just innocent fun, but I assure you, it is of deadly importance. You see, a young man might be hurled into sin just by looking at you in the wrong kind of dress." Father Aimery reached out, and Aurelie numbly offered her hand. He patted it. "I'm sorry to be the one to tell you."

Aurelie released a shuddering sigh. "Thank you for letting me know," she said. "I will be careful."

"Very good," Father Aimery said. "I was sure that you would see the importance of the matter."

Aurelie didn't answer.

Father Aimery released her hand. "Now, where is my staff?"

Seraphine grinned, pushing in front of Aurelie and tapping the monstrosity of wrapped wool and smeared blood against the stone floor. "Won't you let us keep it, Father?" she said. "As a kind of blessing for the princess on her special day?"

Aurelie looked at the desecrated symbol, and her stomach churned with anger and despair. She knew that Bishop Aimery would try to take it, and she knew that Seraphine would stop him from leaving the tower with such an obvious proof of her treachery. One way or another Aurelie must stop him—or else Seraphine would. "Please," Aurelie whispered. "It would mean so much to us to keep this staff."

"Impossible, mesdames," Father Aimery said. "That is just not the proper use of a holy symbol." He pushed back into the room and caught the staff. Then his face went rigid. "Why is it sticky?"

"I am too embarrassed to say," Seraphine said. "But women's problems happen in a woman's room. I had hoped to clean it before giving it back to you."

Father Aimery dropped the staff and stepped back onto the landing. "Say no more," he said. "I will use another staff for the ceremony tonight." He reached out a hand, and when Aurelie reached back, he wiped his fingers on her sleeve. "Au revoir, Child. God be with you."

Seraphine closed the door and locked it behind him. Aurelie wiped her bloodstained hand on her dress. Seraphine looked at her and smiled. "Still think God cares to stop me?"

9

The Token

The descending sun shone through the lattice of the broken window and cast the tower room in a gigantic web of light and shadow. Aurelie stared at the silhouette of her own form darkening the closed door, and she did not speak.

Seraphine withdrew the key from the lock and slipped it into her pocket. She waved her shard of glass and glared at Aurelie, as if daring her to try calling for help as the bishop's shuffling steps descended the stair. But Aurelie only studied her shadow. Neither her face nor her body moved. The lower tower door scraped shut.

Seraphine relaxed, leaning against the door and indulging in a low giggle. Then she stooped to pick up the bishop's fallen staff.

Aurelie moved. Her hands slammed against the small of Seraphine's back, shoving her into the floor.

Seraphine caught herself and rolled away, grasping at the keys in her apron pocket and reaching for the staff.

Aurelie bent and tore the pin out from the heart of Seraphine's dress.

Seraphine froze, staring up at her and clutching her dress where the pin had torn a hole.

Aurelie strode backwards, kicking her skirt out of the way, moving toward the fire. Her eyes smoldered in the light of the near-setting sun. She held up the pin, pinching the bone shaft between the thumb and forefinger of each hand. "Don't move," she said. "Or I'll snap it."

Seraphine's mouth dropped open, and her eyes bulged.

Aurelie reached the fire and stopped. "All I have to do is break this little trinket right now," she said, "and all your plans are finished."

"It could still cut you," Seraphine said. Her hands tightened around the staff until her knuckles turned almost white.

"It's not a spindle yet," Aurelie said, giving a hard smile. "It hasn't spun wool, and it has no power to curse me. I can just throw it into the fire, like this." She made as if to toss the pin, and Seraphine rolled, flexing to spring, but Aurelie held up her hand, and Seraphine froze.

Aurelie smiled. Then she kicked the stack of peat logs onto the low flames of the fire. "Hear me now, Madame Seraphine," she said. "If you move, then I will snap this little treasure of yours and toss it into the fire. You will try to save it, but I will fight you. And even if you do manage to get past me, then you will still have to pluck the pieces out of the flames before they are reduced to cinders." Aurelie paused, letting the thought sink in. "How long do you think it will take a little trifle like this to disintegrate in ashes?"

Seraphine's face blanched. She trembled with fury.

A swirl of sparks rose behind Aurelie as the peat and bits of debris caught fire. She smiled. "Even if you do manage to save it, you will still have to make it spin thread before the sun sets, before they come for me and before I walk away from you forever."

Seraphine moaned. Her body drooped toward the floor.

"You have lost," Aurelie said.

Seraphine looked up, glaring at her with unmasked hatred. Then the look changed, folded, her face gathering into wrinkles, her eyes getting lost in the scrunching skin. "Have I really lost?" she said in a soft, sing-song voice.

Aurelie's face remained closed.

Carefully, Seraphine lifted herself away from the floor.

Aurelie stiffened, but she did not break the pin or throw it away.

"Mon lapin, mon agneau," Seraphine said. "I know these tactics because you learned them from me. You are setting me up now, aren't you? You want something. From me. That's why you're still only talking." She rubbed her hands together and rose to her feet. "Let's bargain," she said.

"Call off the curse," Aurelie said. "That is the only thing I want from you."

Seraphine shook her head. "Not true," she said, patting her apron pocket. "You also want this key."

Aurelie frowned.

Seraphine struck the bishop's staff against the floor. "You know I can't call off the curse any more than I can tell the moon to stop rising or the mold to stop spoiling our food. I already told you that." Her eyes narrowed. "So what is it you really want?"

What do you want more than anything else in the whole world? Father Aimery's words flashed through Aurelie's mind. She glanced out the window and saw the sun, glowing like an orb of fire, hovering just over the tops of the hills. She was close, so very close. She was poised to win. But she had to make sure that she understood what winning would cost her. She had to make sure that in winning she did not lose everything. Her face hardened. On the inside, her heart was pounding. "If what you say is true," she said, "then call your gods." She would not say, Call the Devil. "Call them to this room, this hour. Prove to me that they exist. Prove that the curse is real. And then ask them to call it off."

Seraphine raised her eyebrows. "That's what you want?"

Aurelie made a face of disgust. "Are you afraid they won't come?"

Seraphine shook her head. "I'm not afraid of that."

Aurelie searched the older woman's face for weakness, for truth. "My motives are pure," Aurelie said, "so I am not afraid to pursue this option for the sake of my people." She hoped that what she was saying was true. She understood that she was gambling with her life, with her soul and with her kingdom. She told herself not to lose. "This is my proposal," Aurelie said, "if the curse is real, and if someone comes to answer your call, and if they will not simply call off the curse, then we will make a new bargain—one that serves all of us."

"Hmm," Seraphine said. The sound rumbled in the back of her throat. Her eyes had closed to slits. "Are you sure you don't want to just go with the old plan? It might be easier for you in the end."

Aurelie's brown eyes glinted with sunlight and fire. "Either we move forward together," she said, "or I will make sure that you lose everything—starting with this." She held the hairpin so close to the fire that the heat of it stung her hand.

"I accept," Seraphine said quickly. Her eyes glittered, and a smile passed over her face. She set down the bishop's staff in the middle of the room. Then she took the wheel and cord and placed them there too. "Come here," she said, beckoning and pointing to the pin clenched in Aurelie's fist. "That should be in here too."

Aurelie took a step closer. She kept her skirt gathered up, ready to fight, ready to leap back toward the fire, but her body trembled with exhaustion. She could feel her heart pumping like the slow beat of a drum, and now and then it lagged. Now and then it missed a beat.

Seraphine lifted her face. Then a wailing sound issued suddenly from her throat. Aurelie jumped, and the hairs stood up on the back of her neck. Seraphine raised her arms, turning jerkily as she continued the weird melody. She swayed, reaching and grasping at the air. Her body and voice warmed up, creating a song and a dance with an ever-changing rhythm and pattern.

Aurelie clenched her fists, breathing rapidly, trying to keep her composure.

Seraphine danced in a slow circle, passing around the room, encircling the spinning tools. Aurelie countered her movements, keeping a distance, holding the pin always just out of Seraphine's reach. Then, without warning, Seraphine flung up her hands, and her body went rigid. Her large, hazel eyes slowly rolled toward the back of her head till nothing could be seen but a bloodshot white.

Aurelie shook with fear.

A wailing moan erupted again from Seraphine's throat, and she trembled as if shaken by the earth itself. "O, gods of the Jura," she said, and her voice deepened like a growl. Another jerking spasm shook her. "Come now and listen to me! I, Seraphine—spinner of magic, mother of the king's first child, sorceress, survivor and summoner—call upon you now to stand witness to the deal we made sixteen years ago today, the bargain for the blood of a princess."

Aurelie's stomach dropped, and she wanted to fall down and cover her face, to cover her whole self. She wanted to take back her challenge. But she forced herself to look toward the door and the window, to watch for what—for who—might enter.

She saw nothing.

She heard nothing.

She felt nothing.

And that sense of nothingness made her veins pump cold with fear and her skin tighten as if a thousand tiny bugs were crawling across her flesh. She did not feel the presence of something coming into the room. She felt the sense that life was leaking out of it. The fire dimmed and choked and grew smoky. The air, which had blown through the broken window with a strong, fresh breeze, now stilled and grew hotter. Even the sounds of the people outside muted. The light dimmed. Aurelie felt compressed on all sides by a gaping, heart-rending sense of nothingness.

Seraphine's jaw snapped down, and she straightened, slowly and stiffly. Her eyes blinked and returned. "The girl has questioned the validity of the curse," she said. Her voice kept that strange, growling quality. "She wants us to call it back." A smile curved her lips as she listened, holding perfectly still.

Aurelie heard nothing.

Then Seraphine shook, rippling, as a sound of harsh, rasping laughter filled the room. Aurelie realized only after a little while that it was Seraphine herself laughing. "They say, no," Seraphine said. "They say they are thirsty for the blood of a princess." Her eyes gleamed. "Any princess will do."

Everything inside of Aurelie urged her to run, urged her to yell and toss the pin in the fire and fight with every last breath she had to escape this room and this horrific plan. But she did not. Because now, beyond the shadow of a doubt, she finally knew that the curse was real.

Seraphine grasped for the pin. "Give it here," she said. "Be a good princess."

"No!" Aurelie shouted, pulling away. She stumbled back toward the fire.

"Do you want your people to suffer in your place?" Seraphine said. Her voice sounded menacing. "Should I tell the gods that you have abandoned the Free People, and you wish them to be cursed in your place?" She sneered. "Or maybe we should find another princess to play the part. Maybe one of those paragons from your father's precious Zagwe?"

"No!" Aurelie said. She searched her mind, seeking a means to resist, to survive. There is always another way. She had told herself that a thousand times across the chessboard from Seraphine, and so many of those times, when the stakes were not so high, she had found it. She had won. She told herself now that she could win again—one more time.

Seraphine reached for the pin. "Give it to me," she said.

"Not yet," Aurelie said. She thrust her hand over the fire so that the flames brushed her fingers. She tried to keep her hand there a moment longer, taunting Seraphine, and then she cried out and drew back, cradling her hand, still holding the pin, against her body. Her hair tumbled over her shoulders, and her jaw clenched with pain, but she squared her shoulders and drew herself up. Her voice found strength. "I am Aurelie, Princess of the Free Country, and I will do what

I must to save my people," she said, eyes burning. "But I am no pawn in your game. I will make a move of my own first."

Seraphine didn't answer for a moment. Her eyes widened, almost sadly, and her mouth opened, as if about to speak. Then it snapped shut, and a mask fell over her features. "Very well," she said. "Choose your words carefully—more carefully than I did."

Aurelie staggered forward. Her dress felt heavier than ever, no longer swishing but dragging her toward the ground. She raised the pin in her clenched fist. "Gods!" she shouted. "Devil!" Her voice felt dry beyond parching, beyond thirst. "If you want my blood, then you must give me what I want first. You must meet my own demands—the demands of a princess."

No one answered.

Aurelie's legs buckled, but she caught herself and pushed back up. She focused on her fears, hardened herself in them. She did not want to fail as the leader of the Free Country. She did not want to go out of this tower only to meet her people and lead them to destruction. "First," she said, "I demand that this curse must fall on no one but me. If I fulfill my end of the bargain—if I spill my own blood on the spindle—then you must agree that the debts of the Free Country and of its rulers will be paid." Aurelie's brain was swirling, so dizzy that she almost fell down, and then she realized that she was turning herself in a circle. She stopped and willed her feet to plant, her head to rise.

"Go on," Seraphine said.

Waves of dread washed over Aurelie, and a voice inside her head seemed to be telling her that she had done enough, that she should stop there, that she should just prick her finger and lie down and go to sleep. But the thought of that endless, deathless sleep terrified her, and she balled her hands into fists and went on. "Second," she said, "I demand an end to the curse."

Seraphine cocked her head. "They are listening."

"I do not accept this curse of eternal sleep," Aurelie said. "My bondage must have a limit. It can last no longer than—"

"One hundred years," Seraphine said.

"No," Aurelie said, shaking her head. "That's too long."

"Do not think that you can bargain with gods and give them nothing," Seraphine said. She held up a crooked finger. "Remember the Free People. Remember who you are and what you are bargaining for."

Aurelie's chest heaved, and her head sagged. "All right," she said. "I agree to this bondage for the term of one hundred years."

Seraphine nodded.

Aurelie trembled. She felt weaker and more alone than she had ever felt in her entire life. She wondered if this was what it would always feel like, suspended in a cursed sleep, in the care of that nothingness. Then she pushed herself to keep going, to finish the bargain. "Third," she said, struggling to raise her head, "I demand that the curse can be broken."

A low growl escaped from Seraphine. "How?"

Aurelie searched her mind, but all the thoughts seemed to have emptied out of it and been replaced by nothing. Nothing. If she'd had any kind of a plan once, she couldn't remember what it was. She could hardly remember her own name. Her whole body shook with exhaustion and dread and with grief over what she had already bargained away.

"Blood," Seraphine said.

Aurelie heard it dimly. She fell to her knees, clutching the sharp pin in her hands. She seemed to hear raucous laughter close by, then far away, then close by again. Her heart pounded heavily, and she wanted to say yes, to say anything that would end the horror of this moment.

"Blood sacrifice is the only way to break a curse," Seraphine said, her voice muted and distorted, as if coming from far, far away.

"No," Aurelie whispered. "Not blood. Too much blood already." She did not know whose blood she was talking about. She pushed off the ground, trying to rise, but the weight of the dress encompassed her, dragged her back down. "Not blood," she whispered. "Something else. Something good."

Her hair rustled.

She felt a soft touch on her cheek, like the caress of a friend.

The wind blew against her face, refreshed her lungs, and for a moment, the nothingness parted. Aurelie looked up and took in a deep breath. Her mind cleared. "Love," she said. She surged to her feet. "Love will break this curse."

"No!" Seraphine said. "Love is not a way to end a curse. Blood must be paid for with blood. You must trick someone else into taking your place. That's the way to do it. Make it specific. Name a ritual. Name a token."

"No," Aurelie said, a smile spreading across her face. "Only love will break my curse." She turned to feel the wind full on her face, to breathe in its strength, and she saw the broken gap that had once been a stained-glass window, and she remembered that one saint there had had a happy ending. "If you want a token," she said, "then let it be a kiss."

"That's too easy," Seraphine hissed. "I do not agree. They do not agree."

Aurelie let her breath release in a sigh. Her hands relaxed, and she felt something hard start to slip out of her palm. She closed her fist around it, though she did not remember why the thing mattered, why she did not want to let it go. "All right," she said. "Then let it be the kiss of a prince."

There was silence, and Aurelie waited for Seraphine to argue. But instead she heard a thin, piercing moan, a wail of exultation and desolation. It grew until Aurelie covered her ears and dropped to her knees, and a cry tore from her own heart. The heat intensified, like a hot exhale on her face. Then, with a snap, it ended. The sense of nothingness was gone.

Outside, the roar of life returned. Guards shouted. Armor clanked. People were being herded into some kind of order. Inside the tower room, the fire gulped and spurted. The wind blew steadily against Aurelie's face, but it carried with it the dim sound of a moan, and it gave her no comfort. Aurelie thought she smelled roses, but she wasn't sure why or where they were coming from.

A bitter smile twisted Seraphine's lips. "You are aware that there are no princes in the Free Country?"

Aurelie nodded.

"I see you assess your worth highly," Seraphine said.

Aurelie said nothing.

"Well, anyway," Seraphine said. "They agreed to your bargain."

Aurelie nodded, though she hardly cared. She felt so tired. She felt as though the thing that was supposed to happen had already happened, as if something had been taken away from her and was gone. But she tried to tell herself that she had won. She was not just a pawn in other people's games. Or if she was a pawn, then she had crossed the board and become a queen, the decider of her own destiny. She had considered all her options, and she had made the choice to protect her people, and it was the right one. She had done her duty as a princess.

Seraphine reached forward and gently prized the hairpin from Aurelie's clenched fist.

10

Checkmate

The sun sank, low and red, kissing the top of a distant mountain. Aurelie watched it, waiting, though she hardly remembered why. She only remembered that this moment meant something to her. And she was captured by its beauty.

A wooden object was placed into her hands, and she felt Seraphine guide them, showing her how to turn the thing. Aurelie glanced down and realized that she held the food platter—the wheel. It was bound by a rope to the hairpin, and Seraphine was tying her cord of wool from the staff onto the pin. Aurelie gripped the wheel and gave it a turn. The rope slipped off, but she put it back on the wheel and turned the thing again. As she continued the motion, her fingers began to take to the work, spinning the wheel and balancing the tension of the rope so that the hairpin would spin. The monotony of the challenge dulled the pain of her shattered spirit. It seemed that agreeing to Seraphine's plan had been the easiest way after all. Aurelie only wished that she could lie down now and go to sleep.

Seraphine's fingers moved deftly, smoothing out the lumpy cord and letting it twist with the movement of the hairpin. The thread wound tighter and tighter, and then, at last, Seraphine let out a yelp, and she wrapped up the spun yarn in a coil around the pin. "It works!" she crowed. "My spinning wheel works."

She started to unravel more cord from the distaff. Then she paused, staring at Aurelie. "It's enough," she said. "It's already a spindle. Are you ready?"

Aurelie nodded, and she smiled to herself, a secret, inward chuckle. One drop of blood was nothing compared to all that she had already lost. And now, somehow, she would welcome a long sleep.

Seraphine sucked in a breath. "It's time." She held up the spindle, wrapped in wool. The ruby cross sparkled under her fist. Above it, the bone shaft jutted its sharp tip.

Aurelie reached out, finger hovering over the point. Her eyes strayed back to the sun, glowing like a living coal, half melted into the mountain. She felt its sunset rays touch and warm her face.

"Steady," Seraphine said. "Don't try to go back on our bargain now."

Aurelie shook her head. "I'm not," she said. "It's just so beautiful. Even prettier than the window." She laughed softly. "Foolish gods! Silly Devil. They didn't realize their mistake. They must not have known. I am not the one who lost today. Because I chose love. And love never fails." She looked back at Seraphine. "I am Aurelie, Princess of the Free Country, and I choose love."

Seraphine's face hardened. "Do it."

"Caritas numquam excidit," Aurelie said, and she pressed her finger into the spindle.

A single drop of blood rolled down the spike and added its stain to the dirty white wool. Nothing happened.

Seraphine's eyes widened. "Prick your finger."

"I did," Aurelie said. She pressed down again, harder, and she felt the sharp bone of the spindle part her flesh. Another drop of blood oozed down the shaft. She waited for sleep to come and claim her, waited to be relieved of her pain.

The church bell began to clang.

Seraphine's hands, holding the spindle, started to shake.

Aurelie looked at her finger, at the tiny wound, still dribbling blood. Her finger hurt, but the pain was small and measurable. It felt so different from the unfathomable, unbearable pain that rent her mind and heart. She noticed that she did not feel sleepy anymore. She did not even feel faint. A laugh bubbled up inside of her, wild and uncontained, and it burst from somewhere deep and broken and free inside. "I have won," Aurelie said. "I have won, Madame Seraphine. You have lost. The curse has failed."

"No," Seraphine said. Her eyes bulged. "No! My curse did not fail. You are just doing it wrong. The gods need more blood. Prick your finger! Prick it again!"

Seraphine seized Aurelie's hand, and she thrust it onto the spindle. Bone ripped through flesh and tendon, and the sharp point pierced through the top of Aurelie's palm. Aurelie screamed.

The church bell tolled on.

Seraphine held Aurelie, pinned and struggling. But it was the older woman's eyes that widened in horror and her mouth that gaped like a hole. She let go of the spindle, and her body sank slowly toward the floor.

Aurelie looked down at her hand, at the spindle sticking out of both sides of it.

Then bursts of light and sound erupted outside. Aurelie gasped and staggered a step toward the window. War shouldn't be happening now. Her people weren't supposed to suffer. Not anymore. Not after the deal she'd made. Then a jubilant clamor arose, clapping and cheering, and Aurelie recognized the sounds of mass delight. She sagged, relieved. The explosions outside must have been some kind of entertainment—a new trick of the king's, his fondness for a pageant.

Aurelie looked down again at her hand. Her stomach twisted, and she carefully touched the spindle. The pain of her punctured flesh stabbed through her all over again, and she clenched her teeth to prevent another scream. Then she wrapped her fingers around the spindle and wrenched it out of her hand. Shock waves of pain rolled through her body, and she gasped, reeling, holding her breath. Blood gushed from the hole. When she could move and breathe again, she pressed the wound into her skirt and wrapped it in scarlet and real gold thread.

More light-bursts erupted outside.

Aurelie looked down at Seraphine, crumpled on the floor, lit by intermittent flashes of light. The old woman let out a soft moan and closed her eyes. Aurelie bent and pulled the keys from her apron pocket. Then she went to the door, unlocked it and swung it open. She tossed the bloody spindle down the staircase, and it rattled and clacked and stopped somewhere around a curve beyond sight.

Aurelie leaned on the doorframe. She remembered that there should be a pitcher of water for her at the bottom of the stairs, and she longed to go down for it. But if she went down now, she knew that she would not have the strength to get back up the stairs again. There was one more thing she had to do before leaving. She searched through the torn and tousled pile of bedding and retrieved her old leather belt. Then, gritting her teeth against the pain, she looped the two keys through the belt and bound it fast around her waist.

Another thunderous sound erupted, and Aurelie looked out in time to see a flower of sparks bloom in the sunset sky and then drop, fading as they blew away in the wind. She had never seen anything like it. She glanced back at the open door, hesitating. Then she walked unsteadily to the window and looked out.

The shadow of evening had finally covered the courtyard, still packed with people and guards carrying torches. A haze of smoke thickened the air, and a sliver of light, the last ray of sunset, brushed the tower in gold. The dying light seemed to be trying to hold on, burning as brightly as possible for as long as possible. Then it was gone. Just gone. Aurelie's face fell into shadow. The sky darkened toward a horizon of pink and purple clouds, and Aurelie stared at the beauty so impossible to touch or keep, so far from her earthly pain and trouble.

In the dark city below, the church bell continued to clang, as torches lit up, and a crowd gathered in the square. The heralds started once more into the gavotte but were quickly silenced. Down in the courtyard, a hush fell. King Hugh and Queen Yolande were passing through a corridor of guests and toward the stair that climbed up the outer castle wall. The queen had changed into a topaz-blue gown of figured silk, and she wore a silver crown and a large jeweled necklace over her new white wimple. The king had donned a red fur robe and his official ruby-studded crown of gold. His shoes looked longer than the normal length of his feet, and they curled upward in a spiraling point. Along the parapet on top of the wall, the elite nobility had already arranged themselves, clothed in finery and fidgeting quietly as they waited. Father Aimery stood among them, decked in layers of gloriously trimmed and embroidered robes that added a prestigious roundness to all but his slim, jutting neck. He leaned on a new gilded staff, and a golden cord tied his mitre under his chin. A host of other courtiers, noble guests and servants had gathered in the courtyard, their faces turned toward the king and queen, away from the tower. Aurelie did not see Sir Roland. He was probably still guarding some useless post in the corridors. The king and queen reached the parapet and stopped just under the great, faded banner of the silver eagle, flapping stiffly in the wind. All along the castle wall, a row of torches lit up, one after the other. Another fire-flower bloomed in the sky. The crowd cheered. The church bell finally stopped clanging.

Aurelie's breath felt ragged and dry in her throat as she looked at her parents for the first time since Seraphine had spoken all her terrible accusations—since Aurelie had given her own blood to pay off their debt. Now the sun had set, and they had not come for her. Aurelie wondered why. *All they did was lock you in a tower and look the other way*, Seraphine had said. But even if that were so, wouldn't they at least hope she would survive?

The royal couple waved, gathering the crowd's energy. Aurelie watched her parents, standing so straight and regal under layers of finery, and her own legs trembled with weariness. Now that it was all over, now that the curse had been met, she thought about Seraphine's baby, and her stomach seized up as if the wind were being knocked out of it all over again. Aurelie leaned her spent body against the sandstone wall. Had her father—her loving father—really ordered the death of his own child? Had her mother—her pious mother—told him to do it? The king had asked her to overlook his faults that day. The queen had wanted prayer for her soul. Aurelie's eyes burned, dry. Wind whipped the locks dangling over her bare shoulders. Maybe she would not need to forgive them now that her blood had paid their debt.

Behind her, Seraphine pushed off the floor and onto her hands and knees.

Aurelie looked past the king and queen, past the nobles, and gazed down at the people she had waited so long to meet, the people who would soon know her as their future queen. The commoners stood at the bottom of the hill in the open city square. They craned their necks, looking up toward her from that great distance. Could they see her in the darkness, behind the lattice? Could they recognize her face and see the great love she had for them? Aurelie didn't think so. She thought of going out now to meet them even as she was, torn and bleeding. She wished that she could have at least cleaned and bandaged her wound so that she could touch their hands without causing them terror. She wished that she could have had an escort to lean upon. But she couldn't wait for those things. She had to go out of the tower when she herself was ready—that is, when she could gather enough strength to make it down the stairs by herself.

King Hugh lifted his arms. The crowd quieted. "People of the Free Country!" the king shouted, his melodious voice carrying far. His hands gestured with his words. "Today is an historic day!"

Aurelie listened, mesmerized by his voice, by the dazzling movements of his hands, and she sank against the windowsill. She could tell that he loved his people, and they loved him. And even though a part of her doubted him now and judged him, she felt that if she could only get down there to him and stand at his side, then she would find some of the answers she needed, and some of her pain would fade.

She pushed off the sill, standing upright, turning to leave, but the sound of hooves trampling on cobbled streets stayed her feet. Aurelie looked back. That fearsome party from the Duchy had crossed the bridges and entered the King's City. Now the crowd in the square was parting so that the leading riders and soldiers could proceed up the road that climbed the hill to the castle. Wind lifted and unfurled the bright banners of blue and yellow. Aurelie held her breath.

Seraphine crawled toward the window.

"For sixteen years, we have all been waiting for this day," King Hugh said. "Surely, we all remember that the Princess Aurelie—my daughter, my own flesh and blood—was cursed to prick her finger on a spindle today, this very day, by sunset. She was supposed to fall into a cursed sleep, never to awaken again, never to serve you as your glorious queen."

The crowd responded with a collective murmur and groan.

Aurelie clenched her jaw. She understood now that her father believed that his plan had been successful, and she was glad of that, but she wished that he would stop talking about her and simply come for her. She felt a continuous throb of pain in her palm, and the oozing wetness of her skirt told her that blood was still leaking out of the wound with each pulse of her heart. Every muscle and bone in her body ached for her to lie down, to rest, but she would not. She could not. She wondered dimly if she would ever truly be able to rest again.

"We good Christians do not fear magic!" King Hugh shouted. "Neither do we show it any mercy. That witch who cursed my daughter was pure evil, not hesitating to harm a baby in her effort to hurt us. But we remained strong. We responded with force. We banished that wicked woman, and we drove away all the practitioners of magic. We burned their wretched books and destroyed the tools of their craft."

The murmuring of the crowd grew and changed, some sounding supportive, some angry, but Aurelie's attention faded. Her body felt cold and her head and hand burned as though they were on fire.

King Hugh paused, his hand resting on his heart. "The heresy of this attack on our God-ordained throne, our God-formed family, is almost too much to believe." He shook his head slowly. "But today, I stand here to tell you that we have won."

The crowd responded.

Seraphine reached out and touched the back of Aurelie's skirt.

"Good has triumphed over evil!" King Hugh shouted.

Seraphine stroked a fold in the scarlet cloth.

A violent tremor passed through Aurelie's body. Was this what it looked like to win? She laughed painfully to herself, rather than cry. With a surge of exertion, she gathered up her skirt and climbed, kneeling carefully on the glass-strewn windowsill. Bits of glass nicked her legs, but she hardly noticed. She clung to the sandstone wall and rose, trembling, until she stood in the broken window. The wind blew all around her, moaning gently, rustling her hair. Her cheeks burned, and her chest rose and fell with the pain and effort of each breath. She brushed at the lattice, letting it fall away, clearing the space before her face. She would meet her kingdom, her people, with a torn dress, a bloodstained body and a face hardened by survival. But she did not mind that now.

She was a princess. And she knew all the agony and responsibility that came along with that role.

Behind her, Seraphine put a hand on the ledge of the sill and slowly raised herself to her feet.

"Let's feast already!" someone in the crowd shouted.

"Bring out the bread!"

Someone else booed. There was a sound of an outburst and scuffle, as a few citizens beat some others into silence. Armor clanked. Then all was still.

The army from the Duchy continued to ascend the hill.

King Hugh raised his hands. "The story is not yet finished! You see, a rumor existed that we locked our beloved daughter in a tower." His voice cracked—then hardened. "Some shameless citizens have spoken out against us for letting the future queen grow up in such a manner, sheltered but stunted, a gullible target for a determined witch." Hugh cleared his throat. Queen Yolande looked at him, and her gaze was cold and motionless. King Hugh did not look back. "Perhaps you, too, thought you saw her in one of the towers," he continued, forcefully. "The ghost of a child's face pressed against a stained-glass window. The echo of a young woman crying faintly in the night."

Aurelie let out a low, involuntary moan. She could not stop the continuous shaking in her body now.

"We ourselves allowed this rumor to spread," King Hugh said. "It was all part of the plan." He placed a hand on the shoulder of the queen. She stared straight ahead, rigid and silent. Then she raised one limp hand and placed it softly on top of his.

Aurelie put her hand out, trying to find a grip on the sandstone wall, trying to steady herself. She wanted to call out to her father, to make him turn and look at her—to speak to her, not about her. But he did not look. No one looked. Or no one saw.

Behind her, Seraphine twined her hands in a fold of the red skirt and brought it to her face. Her breathing slowed.

"To those critics and naysayers," King Hugh said, gazing to his right and then left at the nobles along the wall, "I say—Ha! Ha! It was all a ruse, a pageant, a terrible game, and my queen and I have played the final move."

Aurelie tore at another chunk of the lattice. She needed to see out. She needed to be seen. The pain in her flesh had crescendoed to a fever that burned throughout her whole body, but the pain in her heart was much worse. Unbearable. Unfathomable.

"You see," King Hugh said, "the princess, our daughter, is alive, well and very much awake. And she is right here among us."

Aurelie told herself to smile and wave, to hide her pain, but it took all her strength just to stand. Why didn't the king come for her? Why didn't he turn and look up?

Seraphine flexed her fingers and placed one trembling hand against the sandstone wall.

"We hid her so well that no witch nor curse could ever find her," King Hugh said. "We hid her in the last place any-one of the Free Country would ever think to look." He held out his hands, and a hush fell over all the crowd as they waited to hear his last revelation, waited to see their princess.

A horse whinnied and stamped, breaking the king's spell. Eyes turned toward the party on horseback. The leaders had reached the top of the hill and halted, orderly and imposing. They were backed by a small army, arrayed across the hill-side, outside the castle wall—outside the open gate. The restive horse, a large white charger, whinnied again, falling out of line with the rest. Its rider, a beautiful young woman in a purple gown, tried shushing the beast and tugging at its reins, but the horse only grew more agitated, sidestepping so that she bounced in the saddle. The young woman cowered, whimpering. A net of pearls glinted in her shiny black hair.

A footman stepped in to calm the horse, while a few of the other riders looked away and shook their heads. Then a young man, clad in thick armor and crowned with a thin circlet of gold, eased himself from his own charger and dropped to the ground, clanking. His face was the color of pinewood, flushed with sunburn, and his dark brown hair swept back in long waves from his face. He reached out, touching the arm of the young woman, still cowering, and she shrank away before looking up, pouting. But when she saw the young man—the prince—her round shoulders relaxed, and her full lips curved in a smile, and she might have been Aphrodite herself, smiling in the face of Adonis.

Seraphine uttered a low sound, deep in her throat.

Aurelie did not notice. She heard nothing, and she felt nothing as she watched the young woman reach down toward the prince and melt into his embrace. The prince pulled her from the horse, and she clung to him, not letting go, until he gave her a light shove toward the open gate. She took a few delicate steps, then stopped. Her brown skin glowed in the twilight, and her purple dress gathered to complement her soft, full form. Only her eyes looked unimpressive as they widened, begging someone else to make the next move.

A score of knights rushed out of the gate just then, and the woman shrieked and turned to flee, but the prince caught her, guided her forward, and the knights dropped to their knees, each offering his arm. The woman glanced across them and chewed her bottom lip. Then she placed her hand affectedly on the arm of the closest one and let him lead her through the gate. Once inside the courtyard, she took in the crowd of people, and she froze. Her escort had to pull her, shoulders hunching, to the base of the wall-stairway. There she balked again and clutched her skirt until a courtier offered to carry her train. At the top of the wall, the attendants withdrew, and the young woman stood alone, eyes fixed on the ground, just a few paces from the king and queen.

Silence gripped the crowd, as they waited to see, to hear, what would happen next. The young woman wrung her hands and glanced over the parapet toward the foreign prince. Then she curtseyed with slow, elaborate grace. She did not look up, but remained stooped, her purple dress flowing around her like the shimmering petals of a violet.

The king and queen looked at her, then at each other, then back at the young woman, still lowered in the curtsey. Behind them, a courtier knelt and held up a golden box. The king cleared his throat, and the young woman flinched. She carefully brushed out a fold in her skirt. Then she peaked up, her lips pursed in a delicate smile.

King Hugh stepped forward, his long shoe landing, by necessity, on the edge of her flowing skirt. He reached out, seeming about to touch the woman's face, and she wobbled, teetering in the long-suspended curtsey. His fingers curled back, not touching her, and they stared at each other, neither moving. The young woman's eyes widened painfully.

Abruptly, King Hugh turned away. He seized the edges of the courtier's golden box, gripping it for the span of several long breaths. Then he reached inside and drew out a thin, silver crown, edged with mother-of-pearl and studded with a single amethyst. Hugh stared down at the crown, and he did not move.

Then, at last, he looked up.

He looked up at the tower, at the broken window, at the woman standing in it, and his face twisted in anguish.

The young woman in the tower held perfectly still. Wind played in her tangled hair. Blood pumped from the wound in her hand. Her eyes burned, but no tears fell, and she made no move. She met the king's gaze and held it, and in that moment, she understood the whole game, and she knew that every person had played it to their best. And she understood that she had lost.

King Hugh dropped his gaze.

A feeling of agony tore through the woman in the tower, as though her heart were being ripped in two. But her heart kept beating. It did not stop. It pumped on and on, and blood coagulated around her wound, and light faded from the pink and purple clouds, and stars brightened, and a stillness came over her, like a soft breath gently blowing out a flame.

King Hugh's head sagged toward the crown in his hands. Queen Yolande gave a choking cry, and she seized it. She darted forward and thrust the circlet of silver onto the head of the young woman kneeling at their feet, the woman who was their daughter, Princess Aurelie. The eyes of the princess widened again, but this time they shone, and she touched the crown, tapping the jeweled front and running her fingers along the wrought silver edge. Yolande took the plump hands, entwining the soft fingers in her own, and she urged the princess to her feet. Then the queen kissed the round, delicate, unmarred fingers of the princess over and over.

King Hugh turned back to the crowd. "My people!" he said. "Let us rejoice! Our story has ended happily. The curse is behind us. Our princess has come home. And we have forged a new kinship with the Duchy!"

A cheer arose. The armor-clad prince smiled and gave a clanking bow. The riders saluted. The king nodded to them solemnly.

King Hugh looked at the princess, and he nodded at her too. Then he held out his hand. She seemed to swell a little, and she placed her hand softly, artfully on top of his. The king looked down for a moment at the hand, barely grazing his palm. Then he closed his fingers around it and tugged the princess forward to look out over the parapet. "These are our people," he said, gesturing, "the people of the Free Country!" He raised his hand, waving, touching his heart and blowing a kiss. "My people," he shouted, "I give you—your Princess Aurelie!"

The crowd went wild.

King Hugh tried to raise the hand of the princess, but the tailoring of her purple gown prevented her arm from lifting above the height of her new crown, and she pulled back, hopping to keep her balance. The king dropped her hand and raised his own, pumping his fists and giving one last shout of triumph: "Let's feast!"

A babbling arose as the crowd inside the courtyard began to surge toward the great hall. The leaders from the Duchy were met and invited through the gate, and the nobles along the wall dispersed, exiting through side stairwells. The king and queen spoke together softly. Father Aimery hobbled toward them. The princess glanced back and forth as the space around her emptied, and she bent her elbow, giving a timid wave. She touched the crown, rubbing the purple amethyst. Then she covered her face in her hands and sobbed.

The young woman in the tower swayed. Her knees buckled. At long last, her mind released into the mercy of darkness, and she fell.

Seraphine caught her.

They sank together onto the window seat, amid the blood and broken glass. Seraphine cradled the limp form and gazed down at the closed eyes, the smooth brow, the soft lips that released a small breath, like a sigh. Then Seraphine clutched the young woman—the woman without a name—to her heart, and she cried.

A Note to the Reader

Dear Friend,

If there's anything I want to say with this book, it's this: You are worthy. You are precious. You have unlimited potential. No matter what you have experienced or what choices you have made, you are still worthy and capable of greatness.

If this story seems dark to you, then know that it's not over—just as your own story still has many chapters and books left. The woman without a name might have been exploited and cast aside by some, but she is a survivor, and this is only the beginning of her story.

I began writing this book eleven years ago while processing the feeling of not getting rescued, of having to change or compromise values in order to survive and then trying to rebuild after that, trying to reimagine a new future after dreams, heart and body have all been crushed.

On and off through the last decade, I continued writing to process my grief and outrage over the lack of compassion and the lack of opportunities for healing in our contemporary society. I felt disillusioned by systems of justice that could be bought, lobbied for and traded on the market. I was angry at systems of protection that sacrificed some people's safety for others. I wanted those getting hurt to have a voice, a name, a say in the shape and future of our national and global bodies of power. I imagined what that might look like, and I wrote it. Like I said, the story isn't over.

In this so-called Sleeping Beauty story, the main character suffers because everyone around her greatly underestimates her value. To some, she is even dispensable. But that's the lie. Not one person is dispensable. Some characters in the story are also persuaded by the realities they've experienced that evil is more powerful than good. But the truth is that good is far more powerful and lasting than evil. Every person has a light inside, and that light is much more powerful than the darkness that constantly, desperately tries to overcome or obscure it. But goodness can have a cost—especially when only a few are standing up for it alone.

The meaning of Princess Awakening is that we all need to rise up and see the worth, the goodness and the power in ourselves and in each other. We need to grow and support the good we see. We need to live with empowered compassion.

On my website, www.PrincessAwakening.com, there's a page called "Take Action", and there I've listed some organizations that support people, especially women, who have experienced trauma. These groups are good places to check out if you need support in your own journey—or if you want to support someone else's. I also talk more there about the trauma of princess tropes and my hope for a change in our collective understanding of that character.

Finally, I love you, and I want to thank you for reading this book, for making space for it. May you be encouraged, whatever your story, to imagine the glorious potential of your own personal destiny and to chase those dreams with all your heart.

Much love,
— L.A. Soria

Acknowledgments & Thanks

Thank you to my readers who were willing to stay trapped in a tower room for a whole book with me. I love you.

Thanks to so many libraries full of research and inspiration. Thank you especially to a few writers: Marilyn Yalom revealed how the powerful queens of the Medieval Period prompted the naming of the chess queen. Margaret Scott encouraged me to play with medieval fashion. Geraldine Heng led me to observe the devastating consequences of the portrayals of skin color in medieval art.

Thank you to Courtney Clay, digital artist, for illustrating so many images of beauty and intrigue. Thank you to Antoinette Scully, sensitivity consultant, who valued this story and helped shape it with care. Thank you to Rosalie Lander, line editor, for swift and honest feedback. Thank you to Juliana Jordan, first-draft consultant, for listening to the story and being willing to challenge every word. Thank you to Nathaniel Soria, my husband and the cover designer, for creating a vision of mystery and wonder.

Thank you to all my friends and family for support, encouragement and sometimes housing and food throughout the eleven years of working on-and-off on this saga.

Thank you to my son for living the nomadic, artistic lifestyle from so very early on and for sharing in the family commitment to making art. Thank you again to my husband, my dearest friend, for being a partner both in practice and in heart. Though the story began without you, you have added to its love, honesty, courage and hope.

Coming soon...

BOOK II
WOMAN WITHOUT A NAME

What's the next move for the woman without a name? To support the continuation of this saga, please visit www.PrincessAwakening.com and buy a book for a friend or make a donation.

CPSIA information can be obtained
at www.ICGtesting.com
Printed in the USA
FSHW011255130521
81431FS

9 781736 134603